The
ETCH
Anthology
2017

Vocamus Press, Guelph, Ontario

Guelph Public Library
Explore • Connect • Thrive

ISBN 13: 978-1-928171-53-9 (pbk)
ISBN 13: 978-1-928171-54-6 (ebk)

Produced by Friends of Vocamus Press

Vocamus Press
130 Dublin Street, North
Guelph, Ontario, Canada
N1H 4N4

www.vocamus.net

2017

CONTENTS

NEWCOMER STORIES

GRADES 11 - 12

GRADES 7 - 8

Sponsors

ETCH 2017 is produced by Friends of Vocamus Press, a non-profit community organisation that supports writing, publishing, and book culture in the Guelph area.

This season our work has been generously supported by Alec Follett, Andrew Goodwin, Jaya James, Sheila Koop, Jane Litchfield, Bieke Stengos, and Janice Wiseman. We appreciate their support very much.

We'd especially like to recognise the support of Kim Lang, whose generosity has allowed us to redesign our website in order to better serve the literary community in and around Guelph.

If you'd also like to support the work of Friends of Vocamus Press, you can do so by searching us on www.patreon.com.

Preface

The stories in this collection are the winners and runners up from the Guelph Public Library's 2017 Teen Writing Contest. They were judged and arranged in the collection by grade level, except for the three winners of this years' special Newcomer Stories category.

The cover of the collection was made using the winning entry of the Guelph Public Library's 2017 Cover Contest, created by Morgan Curtis, a Grade 10 student at Centennial Collegiate Vocational Institute.

Writerly mentorship was provided by local authors – Phil Andrews, Shane Arbuthnott, Avril Borthiry, Daniel Bratton, James Clarke, Douglas Davey, Marina Gascho, Michael Hale, Darcy Hiltz, Karen Houle, Bill Hulet, Kasia Jaronczyk, Michelle Jay, Danielle Joworski, Kim Davids Mandar, Sean McCabe, Claudette Melanson, Rob O'Flanagan, Andrea Perry, Marion Reidel, Greg Rhyno, Karen Smythe, Bieke Stengos, and Robert Young

The Teen Writing Contest was organised by Elissa Davidson of the Guelph Public Library. The ETCH Coordinator for Friends of Vocamus Press was Charly Kirkwood. The stories were judged by Elissa Davidson, Jeremy Luke Hill, and Charly Kirkwood. The book's cover and interior were designed by Jeremy Luke Hill of Vocamus Press.

NEWCOMER STORIES

Sasha

Zaya Stas

"Get in the car honey," my mother said. Her voice was so low that I could barely hear her. It was early in the morning when my family went to say goodbye to my grandparents. I always thought grandfathers didn't cry. I was wrong. My grandfather was standing on the balcony of their house. That was the first and last time I would see him crying.

My grandmother whispered to me, "Be brave my girl." I still remember her standing by the gate trembling like a tree leaf as she was trying to hide her tears. All the way to Lebanon my mother did not speak to me or my siblings. In fact, none of us spoke to one another. Instead, my mom cried until we arrived while my little sister Maya slept.

I closed my eyes and she was there. "Are you okay, Sasha?" I asked. She smiled at me like she always did. "I am with you. Don't be afraid." Sasha was my best friend. I got her when I was five years old. The moment I saw her sitting there on the shelf I knew she was meant for me and I brought her home. She was such a pretty doll with her dirty blond hair and blue eyes. She was dressed in old fashion clothes. She was my hero and I would take her everywhere. She was the keeper of my secrets and now she accompanied me on my journey to a new land.

When we reached Lebanon, I turned my head to see the last sliver of Syrian land: my home. "Take care, Sasha." I left a piece of me with her. I had a lot of questions in my head, but no answers as my father's face looked so serious I knew it was not a good time to ask him, so I kept my questions to myself. "Are we ever going to go back? Why didn't grandma and grandpa come with us? Dad, why are you so nervous and confused? Where is everybody? My friends? My teachers? What is happening to us?" So many questions filled my head. I couldn't understand what was going on around me.

Without warning, we had left our home, our village and now we had left our country. Everyone looked different. My mom kept saying, "Don't speak to anyone and don't answer any questions." The smell of danger was everywhere. Every face I saw had one of two expressions: fear or sadness. In the end, the design was made. We had left and we were here, in Turkey; trying to put our lives together and start again. I was a plant in a foreign land.

Everything was new: new house, new school, new people, new language. It was the beginning of my new life. It was strange to see so many mouths talking and not being able to understand the meaning of the words. My family struggled to learn Turkish, but we succeeded.

"Are you still there, Sasha?" With a smile, she nodded her head.

I keep remembering dad trying to find a job to be able to support our family. Every day he would come back home feeling frustrated and disappointed, without a job. It changed my father. He stopped playing with us and the odd time he would play with us, he seemed distant. He was always quiet and thinking.

One day, he left. I came back from school and he was not there.

My mom had locked herself in her room. My brother and I used to listen behind the door to hear any sound and make sure that she was still alive. In the end, she came out. Dad was no longer there. Day after day, things changed. We started talking to dad on the phone, but every time I asked, "When are you coming back," he didn't give me a straight answer. I figured out that it was going to be a long time before we saw him again. I thought I would never see him again, and I couldn't talk to anyone about it. But I had Sasha.

"Sasha, I'm lonely."

"Don't be. I am with you. I feel you. Remember this time will pass and good days will come."

She was right. Those good days did come.

One day mom told us that we were leaving again, and this time we were going to Canada. My mother told us that this would be our last journey. Soon we found ourselves in another world again, with another language. My mom was tired, but glad. I could tell from her voice. "We will be fine," she said. I believed her.

When we arrived the first thing that I thought was: Dad, you have got to see this. And he will, I am sure of that.

"Are you there, Sasha ?" I asked

With a face glowing and shining, she answered, "Yes, my dear. I will always be here for you."

The Power of Bonjour

Kyla Wilkinson

Throughout my years as an elementary student I was bullied and had troubles with friends treating me terribly. I would make new friends, and the process would repeat itself again. I would come home crying, telling my parents what horrible things my "friends" had done to me that day.

Then I decided I couldn't handle being in the same class as these people who were once my best friends, and in the same school as the other students who bullied me. I felt like there was no one else for me to try and make friends with, and I needed to get away from these negative people. That's when I started a new chapter in my life.

In the middle of Grade 7 I decided to switch schools. My mom was a teacher at the same school I went to. She was talking with my French teacher one day, and my French teacher told my mom how she thought my French was strong enough to switch from Core French to a full French school. There were no full French schools close to us that I would have been able to go to, so we decided to go to Erin Public School.

My mom and I drove into Erin for an interview. The principal interviewed me and we talked in French. It was unheard of for someone to switch from core French to French immersion, let alone in Grade 7. After talking, showing him some of my work, and touring the school, he thought my French was strong enough to switch. So after the Christmas break I had my first day at my new school.

The first day I came to Erin Public School I was very nervous. I came to Erin in January, so by then everybody in my class was already used to the school and most of the kids in my class had known each other since kindergarten. My Mom drove me to school on the first day so that I would feel more comfortable. She introduced herself to my French teacher, and he showed me where my locker was. I was so nervous after my Mom left.

I was standing by my locker when a girl at the next locker introduced herself. I remember being so glad that somebody started talking to me. Then we headed to the gym, I was very confused. Two other girls explained what was going on, and how we worked out every morning. That took some getting used to! My first thoughts were: "Wow everyone here is so friendly!".

At the end of the day my teacher had to help me find which bus I was taking because I didn't know. The first day was very overwhelming but after awhile I got used to things. I talked to my parents about how my first day went, and the one thing I will always remember about my first day is how nice everyone was to me. I made friends quickly and felt so welcomed by everyone – they were eager to get to know me. I joined band, art club, cooking club, student council, and a few other clubs. There were so many more opportunities available to me at my new school.

At the end of the year I received my report card, and I saw that I was only a few percentages below the class median in ALL my French classes. I recognised what an amazing accomplishment I had made. Catching up to my peers in less than six months was a pretty spectacular thing indeed! I was not as strong as the kids who had been in French Immersion their entire life, but with hard work and determination I could be in French Immersion.

Fast forward a year, and I was getting ready to go to France.

I always knew that I wanted to go to France ever since I heard about the ISE (International Student Exchange) program back in Grade 6. I had always had a love for French. I won the Grade 6 Core French award, and being in French immersion definitely improved my French a lot. I was feeling confident, and excited to go to France. I would be staying in France for twelve weeks, and today was my eleventh day at school.

Before I started school I was on vacation. My exchange partner and I visited Paris and Versailles! It was really cool to go to so many different places since this was only my second time out of Ontario! Being on vacation before school helped a lot since I got to hang out with my exchange partner and get to know her before I started school.

Things were very different in France compared to Canada. I woke up at 6:40 to the sound of my alarm clock beeping. I got dressed and had breakfast. While I was getting ready for my first day of school I was feeling a little anxious. At 7:45 we were out the door walking to the bus stop in the pouring rain. The public bus picked us up and I used my new bus card to get on the bus. Then after we got off the bus we went into the office at my new school. I got my schedule and a book that you need to get in and out of the school, the teachers need to make sure that you don't leave before your classes are over.

My school in France was definitely bigger than my school back in Canada. There were lots of stairs, and over 700 students! After I finished my tour I went with some other students into a class called a permanence. You go there when you don't have any other classes. In permanence you can't talk, so you have to be quiet and do work. My exchange partner and I just played tic-tac-toe. As time passed, and my first class was getting closer and closer, I was feeling more anxious.

My first class was technology, I was a little lost since I don't have this class in Canada. I met all of Inès' friends. They were extremely nice! So far I was understanding the French. It's a little hard to understand when many people are talking the same time and talking very fast, but I'm getting the hang of it!

Then my next class was English. The teacher loved me! For the entire class I stood in front of everybody and they asked me questions in English about my travels to France.

Then it was time for lunch. You have to enter your code and scan your hand on a machine, but we hadn't set this up for me yet so one of the administrators gave me a tray for my food. Then you get to pick out your food. It's very fancy! You pick out an entrée, your main dish, and a dessert. Then we sat down for lunch, Inès' friends made me feel very welcome, and I was very glad about that since I was pretty nervous.

Then we were supposed to have math, but our teacher wasn't there, so we went to permanence instead. Then we had physics-chime, I don't have this class in Canada either. We were working on the mass of air.

Then the day was over, we took the public bus home. They have a lot of homework in France. Inès and I did it together. Then we ate some dinner and went to gymnastics. It's also very different from when I do gymnastics in Canada. With my first day over I talked to my mom and dad about how it went. I was feeling very happy with my day, and I could already see my French improving!

As overwhelming as my first day, week, and two weeks were, they were such an amazing experience and I'm so grateful. By the fifth week of school I felt like I had a place with the group of friends, and I was participating more in class discussions. My French was improving immensely, and everybody wanted to get to know the Canadian girl, so I didn't ever have to have a problem of no one talking to me.

Within two years I'd had two experiences about being a newcomer – one switching to another school, and one switching to another school in another country where everybody speaks a different language. These experiences changed my life greatly and helped me become the person I am today. I believe everything happens for a reason, and as terrible as the experiences I went through with my friends were, they all taught me something. Those experiences led me to greater experiences and allowed me to meet people who played a very important role in my life. The experiences I went through with my friends led me to being a newcomer – twice! And during that time as a newcomer, I learned so much more about myself.

The One Rupee Coin

Pooja Sankar

Right as I began to ease back into my chair after my very first day of work, some memories began to rush back to me. I thought of all the places I had been. I pictured the most beautiful sights I had seen around the world and the most memorable moments I had experienced. Yet for some reason, I thought back to the day I arrived at the airport on one of the coldest days in December. I just couldn't get myself to believe that this was almost ten years ago today.

I stepped out into a stormy winter night without the realisation that this step was my very first one into a new life. I can still remember my mother's hopeful face as she kissed my forehead. As she stood above me, I felt a single tear roll down her eye and make its way to my cheek. I stood there silently in sadness. My mother took both my hands, placed a coin in one of them and held them tightly together while bringing them close to her chest. "I could not be any more proud of you. All I ask is for you to find happiness in Canada. Make it your home. Here, with me, this will always be your home. I'm not going anywhere. Don't worry about me because I know you will. I will be right here when you come back. I'll be right here waiting. Your joy is my biggest gift. Take this one rupee coin for good luck. I know that you will create a great future for yourself. Remember that the most rewarding feeling is the one that comes from doing what you love and the moment your hard work begins making a difference in others' lives. There is no greater sense of satisfaction than that which comes from following your dreams and aspirations. I cannot wait to see my beautiful son grow up into a generous and kind man. I love you, sweetheart."

At the moment in my life I felt more proud and confident than I have ever been. Every time I feel afraid or alone, I think back on the things my mother always said and, soon enough, I feel a sense of undying hope. My mother always had that effect on me. She was the most hardworking, kind and generous person. She raised us without making us feel the lack of another parent at home. She saw the goodness in others that many of us can never see. Although our family was not financially well off, she never made me feel a lack of anything growing up. My mother was my biggest friend but also my biggest supporter. She was the one who taught me to believe that any dream was possible with hard work and hope.

I threw my heavy suitcases into the trunk of the first taxi that arrived. The wind began to pick up and blew the snow into my loose sweater. I still remember the taxi driver. He said that he was also from India and that he moved to Toronto twenty-five years back. "I'm from New Delhi. I'm a civil engineer. Actually, I used to be one back home." The rest of the trip, the taxi driver shared many of his favourite memories of home. He talked about how much he missed chai and the hot fried snacks sold at road sides for a cheap price. Hearing these stories, I just laughed and nodded. I didn't know that soon it would be me in that exact position, nostalgic about the small pleasures back home.

When I reached the apartment building around midnight, I felt surprisingly energetic. I stood by the balcony, looking up at the starry sky, more hopeful than ever; I was ready to start a new chapter in my life. Little did I know all the obstacles ahead of me. I sat down in an empty living room and felt around for my pants pocket. I brought out my one rupee coin and played around with it while thinking of what my mom must have been doing at that exact moment and how much my brothers must have been missing me. As I began unpacking my clothes, I could feel that same comfort as if my mother was right there beside me. I remembered the days my brothers and I spent outside in the boiling hot weather, drinking from coconuts and playing our own version of hopscotch. My suitcase smelled like home and I felt good knowing that I always had it if I started to miss being home. Little did I know that the smell would wear off in about a week and that I would be left with nothing but an empty suitcase to remind me of all the little things that I missed. As I opened my suitcase, I saw that there was a wrinkled letter squeezed tightly between my sweater vests and cotton pants. It read:

> *My beloved brother,*
>
> *Mom doesn't know that I put this letter in when you were both busy talking. I hope you read this only upon arrival. I really miss you now that you're gone. Mother said that she has really high hopes for you. But she also said that she does not want you to know that because she fears that it will seem as though she expects great things. Mother really believes in you and so do all of us. You've always saved every rupee that all the uncles and aunties gave us. You have the intelligence and ambitious nature to be successful. Most importantly, you also have the kindness and generosity to be a good man. We look up to you and we always will. You're so brave for making this journey on your own at the age of twenty-five. Write to us whenever time allows.*
>
> *Love,*
>
> *Ram*

Right before I ease into my hospital chair after my first day of rounds, I go to hang my white coat on the rack. I grab the one rupee coin from the coat's pocket and bring it close to my chest and sit down. Ten years ago today I came to this country. The number of jobs I held are countless. The amount of times I've been discouraged from continuing on this path and following my passions are innumerable. Yet each time, I thought back to how hard my mother worked to get me here. I thought back to how proud she must be, just for my being here. I can picture her kissing my forehead and saying, "I love you, sweetheart." This always pushed me to strive harder and harder all throughout these ten years to get my white coat; my biggest aspiration. And now, it has finally happened. And although there are many out there whose paths turned and instead had to head to new destinations like the taxi driver, I'm still happy for him in that he found happiness with what he had. Mother was right: there is no greater feeling than of helping others, working hard and doing what you love most.

GRADES 11 - 12

Perfection

Ellen Zhang

Jena was disappointed.

She was disappointed in herself and Kieran. Not in their general relationship, but in their story. She was disappointed in its unoriginality, its lack of imagination and the no-risk factor. They were like every other couple in Canada, perhaps every other couple in the world.

They met in high school. They had been in the same class, had shared mutual friends, had spent time at the same cafeteria. They had always seemed to be inexplicably forced next to each other. It was inevitable that their friends would eventually try to get the two together. And equally just as inevitable that they would fall in love.

At their friend's insistence, the two started dating. They went to movies, for strolls in the park, and out for dinner. Sex came spontaneously after a few months – after all, they were teenagers and hormones were rather convincing. And then they fell in love. They couldn't help it, really.

When college rolled around, they both attended the same school, and moved into a cheap apartment together. They fought, just like any other couple. They argued over grocery lists, over Jena's habit of always spending a little too much and Kieran's habit of never spending quite enough.

Sometimes Kieran slept on the couch. Sometimes Jena stormed off in tears to sleep at Abigail's house. But they never had reason to leave one another for good. So they stayed the same, always unchanging, Jena and Kieran, the typical high school sweethearts.

But Jena wasn't happy with the sound of that. She didn't want to be typical. She wanted to be original. When people asked, she wanted to be able to tell them that Kieran had saved her from a near death the first day they met, that they fell in love and had lived happily ever after ever since. Not that they used to share pens in third period chemistry and that their first date took place at your common, everyday burger joint.

It had nothing to do with her actually being unhappy with her boyfriend or bored with their life style. It was just that when she thought about it, she wished their relationship was a little less generic.

So one day, on one of their ordinary strolls through a park not far from home, Jena vocalised her thoughts.

"Kieran, do you ever wish we were less boring?" she asked as they walked along, hands swinging rhythmically between them. She didn't know why she said it, didn't know why she felt like it was such an important thought. He seemed blissfully happy with the way they were.

Kieran glanced at her. "What do you mean? We just went to Disney last week. And we went out for drinks with Ryan and Iris last night. We do plenty of entertaining, un-boring things."

Jena sighed because that wasn't what she meant. Kieran didn't understand.

"No, I mean that we are boring. As a couple, in the grand scheme of things, compared to all the exciting couples of the world. Don't you ever wish we weren't so... conventional?"

Kieran just smiled helplessly and Jena knew that he still didn't understand her. "So, do you mean that you want to have some sort of spontaneous adventure? Go rob a bank or something?"

18

Jena ran a hand through her hair in frustration. "No, it's just that – I don't know. I feel like we never had that epic romance movie type of first meeting. Love didn't come suddenly, it built up over time. I just always dreamed of the whole Prince Charming sweeping me off my feet, love at first sight, fatefully meeting the day of a catastrophic accident, I-thought-he-was-an-angel sort of thing," Jena explained desperately, willing her boyfriend to comprehend. "It's not that I regret falling in love with you, I just sort of wish it had happened differently. I wish Jena and Kieran's love story featured some sort of excitement."

Jena stopped walking, gripping both of his hands.

"But you excite me," Kieran tried, squeezing his girlfriend's hands tightly.

Jena was sure her disappointment was evident.

The awkward atmosphere between them was almost tangible as neither uttered a word. Neither of them really knew what to say. So they stood there, looking at each other, one pleading, and the other helpless.

After a moment, Kieran seemed to give in.

"Alright, run ahead," he said, unclasping his hands from Jena's and nodding in the direction in front of them. "Run ahead and pretend to fall down." He pushed her forward.

Jena gave her boyfriend a strange look. She had no idea why she was being told to run ahead and fall down. It didn't make much sense to her. But nonetheless she went, because Kieran was a fool and Jena was willing to play along.

"Make sure not to fall too far from that bench," he called out once Jena had made it about a hundred yards away.

She realised that said bench was just a few strides away and immediately dropped to the ground, crossed her legs, and looked over her shoulder to stare at Kieran expectantly. She was a little embarrassed from the passers-by who were staring at her, but she was more concerned with figuring out what her boyfriend was up to.

19

Kieran just stood there for a moment as a lazy grin slowly took over his handsome features, and then he was off, jogging in dramatic slow motion towards Jena, hair whipping around in the breeze.

Jena thought she would to die of embarrassment when Kieran knelt down next to her, fake panting and wiping non-existent sweat off his brow.

"Are you alright?" he practically screamed as he reached out a hand to clutch Jena's wrist.

"Of course. You told me to –"

"Oh no! What ever shall I do? Your knee is bleeding uncontrollably! It must have been injured in the fall. You have to let me help you before you bleed out and die!" Kieran went on dramatically.

Jena looked down at her legs. Nothing was bleeding as far as she could tell. Obviously her boyfriend was going delusional. But she supposed it was entertaining enough. She looked at Kieran, faking a pained expression and whimpered that it hurt and that she would be thankful for some help.

"Help me stand you up so that I can sweep you off your feet," Kieran stage whispered, urging her upward with a tug of the sleeve. Jena stood uncertainly to humour him.

"Do not worry, princess," Kieran declared as he swept her into his arms bridal style, successfully pulling a shriek of surprise from her lips. "I'll save you. Fear no longer for your life."

And with that Kieran walked Jena, the whole two strides, to the bench, gently setting her down.

"Now just allow me a moment to retrieve medicine and bandages from my pack," he said, tugging Jena's small backpack away from her, rustling through it before pulling out a half empty water bottle and a blue sweater.

Jena watched in confusion as Kieran unscrewed the cap of the plastic water bottle and poured a meagre amount onto Jena's jean clad knee, all while muttering about how it was extremely lucky that he'd found the other on the brink of death, all bloody and bruised but still beautiful, he added hastily and arrived just in time to save her life. It must have been fate, he said. As if some greater force had brought them together. Jena chuckled as Kieran wrapped the blue garment loosely around her now dampened jeans.

"And there you are," Kieran concluded softly, gently patting the mound of bundled cloth. "You're safe now, no need to worry any longer."

Jena finally understood what was happening. She stared into her boyfriend's dark eyes, tears suddenly appearing out of nowhere. She didn't know why she felt so touched. "Thank you, sir," she whispered. "How will I ever repay you?"

Kieran playfully pondered the thought for a moment. The answer seemed to come to him suddenly and his face lit up, mouth gaping open. Jena thought at that moment, as she looked at her boyfriend's exaggerated expression, how glad she was that he'd never so much as thought of pursuing acting as a career.

"Your name," he said, enunciating his words meticulously. "I want to know your name."

Jena smiled as best as she could through tears. "Jena," she choked in response, because Kieran was an idiot and they were too old for this and he already knew her name and people were staring. But she loved it anyway.

"Jena," Kieran said, nursing the name on his tongue as if he didn't want to let go of the second syllable. "Beautiful."

And it was there, in front of the stares of clueless pedestrians, that Jena realised she had been silly. She didn't want a relationship with a thrilling plotline. She didn't need an interesting introduction because this was the climax. Kieran was the climax, his loving notions, the highest peak of their relationship. Because Kieran was perfect and a racing pulse was all the excitement Jena could ever want. They weren't cookie-cutter. They were one in a million. Jena and Kieran, one of a kind.

The most perfect man in the world, her own unconventional version of Prince Charming, gripped onto her fingers and looked up at her with the most perfect expression.

"My name is Kieran," he said. "Would you like to fall in love with me?"

Jena laughed through salty tears and reached hands out to run her fingers through soft locks of hair, grabbing gently at the roots as to pull Kieran closer.

"I think I already have."

The Waypoint Under the Moon

Julia Hohenadel

I can't live like this any longer, I think to myself, my mind calling in anguish as I flee into the night. It's too much.

I can't tell what's moving faster, my mind or my legs. I'm leaning towards the latter, as my legs carry me with the grace of a deer, whereas my thoughts grow tangled, tripping over each other as they run circles through my tired mind. I'm lucky I don't have to think about where I'm going; my heart knows the way, and it guides me over the rough terrain, leading me towards the sea. I slow my pace as I approach the shoreline, pausing only to catch my breath.

On this cool summer's night, visibility is low; obscured by tendrils of clouds, the moon has a difficult time piercing the night sky, especially without an army of stars at its disposal. Nevertheless, a woman of the coast can always get a sense of the sea, as though the salty brine coursing through our veins can tell us about the state of the ocean. I can hear the waves washing lazily against the shore, the water having reached a state of serenity that contrasts with the vortex of my thoughts.

Slowly, deliberately, I remove my shoes, trusting no one will be around to take them at this hour, and leave them on the shore. I approach the sea, steeling myself against the cold, and walk into its depths. The frigid water sends shivers up my spine, numbing my body as well as my mind. Soothed, I continue trudging forward, water rising from ankle height to past my knees, until I arrive at a large rock formation jutting out of the surf, appearing as though it's reaching out to the moon. I clamber onto the rock, my frozen limbs too clumsy to produce movements that are graceful, just grateful to have reached my destination. Well, perhaps not my final destination, I remind myself. Perhaps this is only a waypoint.

Perched on the edge of this rock, my legs dangling above the water, I lose myself in my horizon. The cool air carries with it the taste of salt, and breathing it helps purify my thoughts, as though the salt has the power to burn away what's troubling me. The moon has torn away from the clouds now, and it illuminates the water with an eerie glow. It's funny, I muse, how the night can be so clear, while my thoughts remain so muddled.

It's only then, when I am one with my surroundings, that I break down the walls holding back my emotions, quickly realising that releasing the floodgates means something quite literal. Tears trickle down my face, stopping as they reach my chin, seemingly too discouraged by the vastness of the sea to continue their journey. Save for one; in shedding this teardrop I blink, launching it from my eyelashes and releasing it into the sea. I think nothing of this until the area where the drop landed begins frothing, bubbling like a witch's cauldron. Startled, I recoil in fright, not daring to believe my eyes.

From the foam arises a woman, a woman more beautiful than any I have ever seen. Her body seems almost translucent, and her skin glows with a soft yellow light. I know that someone with such an ethereal look could not be a figure of my imagination; there's a quality in her eyes, a mixture of wisdom and vitality, that makes me certain that she is real. However, that doesn't stop me from scrambling back in alarm as she draws close to me.

"I know not thy name, though you know me,
With thine tear I arose from the sea,
Thou art not mad, as it may seem,
Anon, thy thoughts I must glean."

I pause, blinking rapidly in alarm. I must be crazy; this must be some sort of stress-induced hallucination. I could write off the sight of this figure as a trick of the light, a stray moonbeam dancing off the waves, but I cannot ignore the spirit's voice.

"Tush, tush, my girl,
Oh! How thy thoughts swirl,
What you need is to speak,
'Fore the moon hits its peak."

I consider this. It couldn't possibly do any harm to voice my troubles out loud. It seems to me to be the right thing to do before altering the course of my journey.

"My name is Ophelia," I begin hesitantly. "I'm… I've lost my way."

The spirit nods encouragingly, urging me to continue.

"I've done some pretty stupid things… But nothing quite like this. My sister and I are inseparable – we were only apart when she left the womb first. We always said we'd do everything together, we'd share everything…" My voice falters as I fail to stifle a sob. My poor sister. "But I don't think she would've wanted to share her boyfriend with me."

The spirit floats closer to me, as if the wind carries her.

"Love is such a fickle force,
One cannot predict the course,
The journey that love will lead,
Nor the sorrows love will breed."

25

"I didn't want to hurt her, Spirit!" I exclaim. "She means more to me than anyone else! But when he was too drunk to distinguish me from her at the party... I didn't correct him."

I cast my gaze downward, the weight of my conscience hanging heavily on my shoulders. I want to continue to explain myself, to justify why I did what I did, but I know no excuse could make up for what I had done. I don't talk for several minutes, and the Spirit, sensing I am fading away like the tides, tries to coax me back into conversation.

"Thy deeds you must not abhor,
'Tis said all's fair in love and war,"

the Spirit assures. She pauses, then asks,

"My dear, why art thou upon this shore?"

I find the gentle, melodious voice of the Spirit to be quite soothing; with each harmonious syllable I feel myself relax. She is comforting yet insightful, a good listener, and to my delight, she withholds all judgement, focusing instead on consoling me. I had desperately needed this. I stare into her eyes, surprised to see that, unlike the rest of her body, they exude no light.

"I'm afraid I didn't tell you the whole story," I admit.

The Spirit nods sympathetically.

"I'm here because I'm out of options." I pause. "My sister's going to find out sooner or later about what I did... Because, well..." I stammer, realising I've never made this admission out loud. "Because I'm pregnant, and I don't know what to do." I grit my teeth, feeling more tears squeeze out of my eyes. "My sister is the only person who would take my side in this situation, but I can't count on her, not under these circumstances. My family will disown me!" I exclaim as sobs wrack my body.

I gulp down the cool sea breeze, trying in vain to calm myself down. "I'm going to save us all the pain."

The Spirit doesn't speak at first; instead, she stares at me with such intensity it feels as though she's piercing through my eyes into my very soul

"You wish to pass through this world?" wonders the Spirit. I nod in confirmation. Her face lights up with this, and in her eyes I notice for the first time a sinister gleam.

"Now my dear, you mustn't baulk,"

she starts, her speech growing ever more rapid.

"Close thine eyes, let go the rock,
Save thyself from future bleak,
And drift away, into the deep."

And I realise, as I begin to lose my footing, that perhaps this isn't such a benevolent spirit after all. The wind picks up, seemingly generated by the spirit's fervour. I feel myself slowly sliding off the rock, as if I'm being pulled into the water by a force outside of my control. I know I should try to fight back, or at the very least scramble for a handhold before plunging into the sea. But my weary, defeated brain wonders if maybe this is a blessing in disguise. Giving up, submitting to the spirit's will – that might not be the worst way to go out. I grit my teeth, my mind made up, and leap into the water's depths.

The Cosmos is Infinite and We Were Mere Instances

Lily de Loë

The night is cold, and as I exhale, wisps of condensation hang suspended in the air, unfurling like the arms of a spiral galaxy. Each water droplet is a star, scattering light amongst the particles.

It is here, standing on top of my apartment building, that I see the world as it is. From this rooftop, with its chain link fence and asphalt top, I view the people down below as ants. In contrast, the stars above are bright pinpricks of light that should make even the greatest of people feel small. On this rooftop, not even twenty floors up, I am as indistinguishable to those below as they are to me. From space, even our towering architecture appears insignificant. Our mark on the universe is the dim glow of artificial light emitting from a rock, barely noticeable amidst the glare of our sun. We are small in the scale of the universe, and have spent too many centuries believing we were the centre of it.

But my feet are on the ground, and not in space, and for once I must focus on the reality in front of me, rather than the stars. It is the present that I should be describing, because you will be viewing the exact same cosmos as me, long after my generation is gone. Perhaps from a different vantage, sights set on another corner of our galaxy, but it will be our galaxy all the same. I wish to describe the scene before me, because I feel it will be incomprehensible to you. Even the smallest, most mundane detail will seem foreign, just as your life would be to me. But now, I am tasked with attempting to explain it. In this moment, the asphalt is cracked and damp, with water seeping into crevices and pooling wherever the once smooth surface has chipped away. Within every reflection, I catch glimpses of the universe. The face of each pool holds a fragment of the Milky Way, and with the North American power grids shut down for the first time since they were erected, the sky is brighter than most could ever have imagined.

In this newly dark night, everyone, regardless of age, stares gawking as if they are viewing the world for the first time. The children, with their unabashed curiosity, best convey the feelings in this moment. Unlike the couples splayed across a checkerboard of blankets, they feel no need to hide their wonder for fear of seeming ignorant. Take the group to my right, standing huddled around one of the larger pools. They whisper, none daring to disturb the reflection at their feet.

None, perhaps, except for one. A girl, no more than five, is crouched with plump fingers outstretched just millimetres above the pool's face. If she were to touch the glassy surface, would the universe warp at her will? Would the ripples that she created reflect those of the gravitational waves that ripple the very fabric of space-time itself? I doubt that she is asking herself these questions. I doubt that she would even care to listen if I offered to teach her.

I could go on indefinitely about such ripples in space-time, and the concepts of relativity that lead to their hyphenation, but I know that is not the information you seek. If you were as enamoured with physics as I, you would turn to a database, and not some antiquated letter. I am writing this because the sun is dying and you are reading this because you wish to understand what it was like when humanity still inhabited the earth.

Let me tell you what happened to our world, what we did to it with no thought of the repercussions. How politics and the media have such a hold on the public that everything is a conspiracy, a corrupt government scheme set in place to keep power out of the hands of the people. How if the economy could be bettered by the burning of a forest, then it would better to play it safe and burn two. In some twisted way I almost understand where these opinions stem from. The price of water has risen exponentially over the last few decades, and so too has the cost of everything made or grown that requires it. Everyone needed the money, but no one understood that my job was to protect our planet and not to keep them living below the poverty line. Science was considered hearsay until it was too late, and then it was expected to save us.

Here's what they never understood: science saves no one in the end. I chased desperately after it throughout graduate school and my career because science is the study of how every aspect of life functions, and I was fascinated by that. But science does not reveal its secrets willingly, and certainly not to those who mistrust it. In the end, it only gave us time to plot and set in motion a scheme for life on a ship in deep space, its goal to find a new star outside of our solar system.

I wonder how many of the people surrounding me would have hurled the word scientist like a slur at my face in the weeks before the public learned that it was the beginning of the end. How many of them looked longingly at the stars of Hollywood, but disparagingly at the very stars they now hope to live amongst? The tables have turned, and although I'm now friend and not foe, we don't understand each other any better than we did before. We differ in knowledge, and for all of the cosmos, in its vast, romanticised infinity, all I see are stars.

I have never understood the metaphors and the concept

of star-crossed lovers. I cannot share in the awestruck atmosphere when I am so well acquainted with what they are just coming to know. And yet, even as our star dies and burns us along with it, I fall deeper in love with the universe. Maybe that is why humanity has always looked to the stars for poetic inspiration. Maybe the idea of love that is so synonymous with the stars saved us first, and the idea of them as a new home will save us now.

You cannot understand how much I yearn to pass on the burden of this path I've chosen for myself. How it feels to be an architect of humanity's survival, but to be burdened by the knowledge that I will be saving so few. Do those who spurned science understand that a star doesn't die a peaceful death? That ours will expand, taking with it the oceans? I do not wish to live with the knowledge that my Earth will resemble the lifeless inferno of Venus. Maybe, with each word I pen, I am only burdening you with these troubles.

Understand that I have hope for our future, or what you would view as your present. I am not known for optimism – do not think that I believe there is another habitable planet lying undiscovered just a solar system away. There is not. But I do believe in the stubbornness of humanity. You have a ship, a wealth knowledge, and an urgency driving the need for advancement. I stand on a rooftop, and you on a vessel hurtling through space. These people near me on this rooftop will be long gone by the time you read this, either your ancestors or those long forgotten on a fiery rock that used to be home. What was our end is your beginning, and I trust that you'll recognise our shortcomings for what they are: lessons. Earth's end is inevitable, but yours is not.

Know this: alone among any other species on this earth, we watched our clocks tick down till the moment when death knocked on our door and welcomed us into the darkness.

Do better than us.

The Murder of the Musical Lawyer

Jordan Waverman

A woman lay sprawled on the ground in her apartment. It was a nice apartment, all things considered, sparsely furnished but those pieces present were nice, tasteful, Nordic chic (which is to say, almost barren but with that pleasant artificial suburban feel), but this tasteful scene was somewhat marred by the waterfall of blood pouring out of the gaping hole in her chest and pooling about the floor. Her eyes and mouth were open nearly as wide, as if in shock that something so horrific could have happened on such a nice day, as the sunlight twinkled in the air like diamonds.

Detective Murphy Ottern, Canada's second best paranormal investigator and a longstanding, if presently unattached, member of the police force, looked up from where he knelt beside the body. He motioned to the body of Ms. Desdemona Avocat, Pemblyton defense lawyer, and at the violin bow impaled in her chest. "While this is most assuredly tragic, I'm sorry to say it's a little outside my purview."

Officer Morrison of the Pemblyton constabulary stared at him in consternation. "I invited you here, Detective Ottern, because your purview is the strange and unusual. This case fits that bill, I can assure you."

"I beg your pardon?"

"Where, pray tell, is the violin?"

Detective Ottern's expression was, as usual, blank. His eyes searched about for only a moment, before settling on the sole ajar door. He walked over, peered in. The fiddle was hung from the ceiling with wires over a chalk pentagram. At each corner there was a photo, dribbled with blood, with an image of a smiling young person hidden under all the gore. The corners of the room were stuffed with trash… cans, bottles, dirty diapers, a fancy cigarette... Most interesting, given the state of the rest of the apartment. Ottern noted it down for later.

"You were supposed to ask me where the violin was," Morrison complained, walking up, then noted Murphy's fixation on the photos. "Dead. Killed when a tossed cigarette burnt down a derelict house they were crashing in," he simply remarked.

Ottern said nothing, but examined the faces a moment more, and a touch of melancholy entered his face. "I presume you have the file for the house fire?" he commented.

Morrison coughed, embarrassed. "It seems to be… missing."

Detective Ottern sighed, and left the room. He paused, for a moment, looking at the body. "If you would be so kind as to find some kind of a file, or preferably video, from her last court case, that would be much appreciated. Assuming that one is not missing too, I'll be at your station."

Detective Ottern sat in a chair at the police station, sipping coffee from a travel mug. Officer Morrison approached, stopped. "Excuse me, but I believe that's my chair you are sitting in."

Detective Ottern took a long, loud slurp from his mug, and gazed languidly at Morrison in the eye. He didn't move.

"I believe you have something of mine," he remarked, and Morrison sighed, but produced a tape from his pocket and inserted it into the tv table near his desk. It began loading, but did so slowly, such that Officer Morrison had time to reach into

33

his pocket and remove a cigarette. He lit it, despite disapproving looks from Detective Ottern, and stood behind him awkwardly as the video clip began playing.

In it was displayed a stereotypical courtroom, barring the defence lawyer in the centre. She was dancing about with a violin and fiddling, her tunes a throaty tenor and her tune unrecognisable. "Your honour, oh your honour, I can assure you the defendant is innocent… And the jury, oh the jury, for he has an alibi… At the time of the murder he was at a ba-ar, on the other si-de of town!"

And on, and on. It wasn't a bad song, nor was it a good song. But it proved the point: the defendant was found innocent. Murphy paused the video. "You were the arresting officer?" He asked, pointing at an irate policeman at the back of the courtroom in the video.

"Yes."

Murphy considered this, nodded. "Do you know the prosecution? That lawyer can't have enjoyed this."

"No, he didn't. In fact, he enjoyed it so little he moved southwards just to never have a case with her again, for she was Pemblyton's sole defence lawyer."

Morrison stopped, and looked like he was awaiting a response, but Ottern merely steepled his fingers. No response forthcoming, he instead opined: "His son is still about, you know. There were death threats between the him and Ms. Avocat. I can get the file for you…"

"No thanks," Murphy interjected, "I can find it myself." He put down his mug of tastiness and left the room, leaving Morrison relieved.

The records room was dark, and Ottern's movements appeared mere flowings in the shadows. He was crouched near the threat files, but wasn't reading them. Instead he was in the corner, poking a pile of wood clippings, or perhaps ash, or perhaps they were the grime of some fell termite infestation (truly, in the dark, it was hard to tell). He stared at their black fluttering shapes for a minute amidst the darkness, as if considering their essence or trying to comprehend their nature of being. He spent much time in the records room that night, but little of it was spent reading up on any threats.

Officer Morrison left the interrogation room, and the sobbing couple within it. "They had no alibi, nor excuse for the letters."

Ottern nodded, his hands steepled contemplatively. He said nothing. He turned to leave, but Morrison accosted him. "So, what do you think of them? The prosecutor's son looked particularly shifty to me, if you don't mind my saying so."

Ottern pondered his response a moment, carefully. "And his wife?"

Then he chuckled, and resumed walking. "I think I have some very exciting leads. I'll corroborate them, and get back to you after lunch."

Morrison sat in his chair, irate. He checked his watch, again. Murphy should have been here nigh on twenty minutes ago. Morrison had important information to tell him about the recent disappearance of the prosecutor from his home, but it seemed as if Ottern was gone, a mere ghost of a thought.

Morrison lit a cigarette and sat back in his chair, the smoke gently twisting its way towards the ceiling. Unexpectedly, a gloved hand grasped the end of the cigarette, tamping it out. A few glowing embers fell to the ground as the Officer stuttered, swinging to his feet. "Forgive me, Detective. I didn't see you there."

Ottern's face showed a touch of a smile. He motioned to the last dregs of smoke. "Nasty habit. But no, most people don't see me. I tend to be invisible like that. Do you know, in France, they call me L'Apparition?"

"I didn't know you'd been to France."

A moment of silence, awkwardness.

"How can I help you, Detective?"

"Well, coming quietly would be nice."

Morrison froze, and for a moment it looked like he might try bolting, but then he fell in on himself. "How'd you know?"

Ottern shifted. "I first suspected something was wrong when I saw the diapers."

"Diapers?"

"Yes, in Ms. Avocat's apartment. Despite the fact that she was single with no kids, her floor was littered with diapers. This made me wonder if the scene was staged, and I looked deeper at the pile. Then I noticed the cigarette."

He motioned to Morrison's cigarette, still clutched in his lips. "Nasty habit, as I said. But very distinctive, high end. I found a stub in the burnt ruins of the file on the house fire, before it disintegrated on me."

Morrison looked down at the cigarette, now in his hands, and sighed.

"So I began to dig deeper into you and your history. You've only been a police officer for what, two years? Before that you were, if I understand correctly, something of a delinquent. Used to run with a street gang composed of five other members… guess which five? You were also the only one not killed in that fire, and reformed shortly thereafter."

He studied Morrison's face and its many folds thoughtfully. "What I want to know is… How'd she find out?"

Morrison sighed. There was no point in holding back. "She was very good at her job. She began studying the case about a month back, and soon noted my lack of an alibi. The fact that I was the only smoker among our group didn't miss her, either. She threatened to turn me in; I had to stop her. The usual, as you clearly know. I was worried, after, that my detective would find out, so I made it look paranormal…"

"So that a paranormal investigator would be called to take the case." Murphy finished.

"Yeah…"

"Because you thought I'd be incapable of solving a normal mystery and so you would escape unscathed."

Morrison winced. He said no more, however, resigned to his fate, even as he was led off.

Murphy sighed, considered the cigarettes on the table before him, and left the room. It truly was a nasty habit.

The Rat

Hannah Stewart

It is moist in this room. He feels it hanging in the air and beading across his fur. He'd come in here to escape this damp coldness. The mud was protection, but the hole had looked better, and once he realised that his haunches could slip through it with little struggle, he knew it was the best option. He had tumbled down, claws hitting something hard as he landed. This was a sure sign that the dampness would be a distant memory in here.

He was wrong. The wet had crept in soon after. Now he huddles as far as possible from the place he entered, nestled behind what appeared to be a high wall of wood. This should have kept the wet at bay, but it doesn't. He wants to move, but cannot. It is strange in here, shapes stacked on shapes that do not make sense. They appear to be made of more materials that he has never seen before. He wants to explore them, but doesn't know what will happen. He fears bringing on an onslaught of the wet.

He fears something else as well.

The cause of this other fear, the strange, unspeakable fear, has disappeared, but it came on with such great force the first time, he doesn't want to risk provoking it. He will not even think of it.

He focuses instead on the mud that remains. It has stuck underneath his claws, inside the curves of their sharp points.

He wonders if he should attempt to clean them on this material. It is so soft looking, more malleable than normal wood, and he knows that his claws would scrape through it easily, but it's strange, strange like everything else in this room. He shouldn't risk it. But the mud is so wet. Instead of drying, the moisture seems to be accumulating. Soon he won't be able to bear it. He reaches a claw slowly towards the expanse. Tentatively, he touches the tip of a single claw to the material in front of him. It is even softer than he imagined. He sets the next claw in line with the first and...

a thunderous noise from above.

It is as if the room is shaking; some unspeakable force is tearing it to pieces. He withdraws his nails, afraid that this wall will collapse upon him, shocked that it is not shaking from the force of this noise. He scampers quickly away.

The shaking subsides, but this time he knows what to expect. He steels himself. The flash of light that follows comes as a shock, regardless.

The light is followed almost immediately with the appearance of a giant.

It is practically upon him when he realises he has not hidden.

His legs shake with fear.

The giant lets out an infernal noise, high and loud, some sort of war call, or something meant to incapacitate its prey. He runs for cover now, behind a strange, shining, curving object.

He is shocked to see it backing away, back in the direction that it came from.

He wonders if this creature's only virtue is its size. if his hiding has fooled the creature into forgetting his existence. In a moment the blinding light has disappeared along with the giant. His lungs release their held air.

He relishes in the sanctuary of darkness for a few blissful moments...

It begins again – the shaking all around. He knows now that the giant must be causing it; it must know what this will do to him. He wonders why the creature doesn't simply crush him. It could. His teeth and claws are no match for the thing's size. He retreats to the furthest, darkest corner he can reach, wills himself to close his eyes and spare them the coming intrusion of light; yet his fear keeps them peeled wide open.

When the light comes, he chastises himself. Filled with bright white spots as they are, his eyes are completely useless. He blinks; once, twice, three times. The blurry spots begin to coalesce into recognisable forms, and his heart races even faster. The creature is closer than it has come before. It doesn't seem to notice him, but its hulking form is ominous nevertheless.

He cranes his neck to look up at the monster's face, hoping to catch a glimpse of its expression and gain insight into its intentions. The shadows are cast so heavily upon its features that he cannot tell if the creature is enraged or simply confused. What he can tell is that the creature holds a strange instrument in its hands. All wire and wood and bizarrely shaped components, the device seems to awaken within him a deep seated and explainable terror.

Yet, there is a smell – so rich, smooth, salty, earthy, heavenly – the most glorious thing he has ever smelled; and somehow it seems to be emanating from the strange device.

He observes the creature carefully, waiting for some action to explain this unexpected inconsistency of instincts brewing within him. The creature begins to move away from him (thankfully). As he watches, the creature bends down. Now he has a better view of its face, and unexpectedly, it appears terribly focused. This tells him that the creature must be intelligent, and this knowledge sends a shiver down his spine.

The creature carefully performs an almost ritualistic looking movement involving one of the intricate parts that composes the inexplicable object, and then, looking satisfied, it rights itself and retreats, taking the light with it.

He continues to cower in his hiding spot, but soon his curiosity becomes overpowering. Slowly, he inches one paw out from the depths of his corner. Nothing horrific occurs, and this gives him confidence. He is drawn closer to the contraption, picking up speed as he nears it. It is as if he has fallen into a trance. Soon he is charging thoughtlessly towards the tantalising smell.

It is only when his nose is practically touching the smooth, foreign mechanisms of the device that he hesitates. Suddenly every feeling of fear comes crashing back upon him. This object has come directly from the horrific creature. This should be enough to terrify him, but his fear runs deeper still. It is as if the knowledge has been written somewhere long ago in the very material that comprises his bones: He knows, without a doubt, that there is something fundamentally wrong with this thing. The wondrous smell no longer appeals to him; it churns his stomach.

As swiftly as the first spell came over him, a different enchantment takes control of his legs. He races as fast as he can back towards the cold, wet draft that is emanating from the hole he once entered – it feels like an eternity ago. His claws slip and slide underneath him. He cannot get any traction on this unwelcoming terrain.

He collides with the wall. His head spins, but he doesn't hesitate. Mind still whirling, he squeezes his aching cranium through the familiar hole, and the rest of his shaking body soon follows.

The mud lets out a great squelch as his thankful body falls upon it. He collapses with relief.

Behind These Walls

Candace Driscoll

Behind these walls lay black and white photos, war medals, laughter. Anything and everything you can think of. Who are they, who are these people that walk these halls? Men and women of all ages; some who call these walls home, some who call it work, where they fold laundry, or prepare meals in the kitchen, some who call the tiny rooms a place for the old and unwanted. But who are these people and what goes on in their minds?

Betty from down the hall shuffles towards me. She wears the same cherry red lipstick everyday that I can see from miles away. Her hair is perfectly brushed with a beautiful butterfly clip holding back her bangs. She eases past me with nothing more than a glance and a nod, all sorts of confusion clouding her eyes. Yesterday she was telling me stories about her daughter's trip to Europe, and how she wishes she could travel the world one day, and today she has already forgotten who I am.

Most of them don't know where exactly they are, while others realise and want to escape.

"Where's my room? Can you help me find my room?" says Bill who's wearing his bathrobe, his hair dripping with water.

These walls are holding them all in. The true meaning of this place may go unnoticed as others pass through, but its twisting halls and adjoining rooms have influenced my past, present, and future. Whenever I see the words Home for the Seniors, my heart fills with warmth.

Nurses, both men and women, offer all of their career lives to care for others. Some keep records of medications, some brush the residents' hair, their teeth. Others feed the ones who cannot feed themselves. As the clock strikes 5 o'clock, it's time for dinner once again.

"When will my husband be coming to pick me up to go home?" asks Margaret with signs of desperation in her eyes.

"Soon. We'll be having dinner here first, then he'll be by after to pick you up, so you better have a good meal!" I reply with guilt burning inside of my body.

I struggle when they ask such questions. It makes my heart feel as though someone just carved it out of my body and threw it into a smouldering river of lava. Every single person here has a story to tell, and I make a choice to listen. Stories about the purchase of their first home and about their first pet. Stories about what they have embarked on during their time here on earth.

John recalls his experiences during WWII.

"It wasn't the best, let me tell ya that... we were knee deep in mud, lice in our hair, bullet sounds piercing our ears, but I was proud to serve my country."

Sometimes I sit and wonder, who were these people when they were babies, ten-year-old children, fifty-year-old adults? I only know them now as grey haired, gentle souls who require constant care.

My dear old friend, Ruby, is convinced that I am her grand-daughter. I decide to play along with it just to make her feel happy and loved. Her face lights up like a kid's on Christmas morning when she sees me walking down the halls towards her. It breaks my heart when she asks me how my mom is doing.

It's funny how much can change in a matter of months, weeks, minutes. I hadn't volunteered for a month at a time, and came back to a completely different place. Residents I once knew when their minds were completely sound had deteriorated. This occurred only in the time it took for the red and green decorations and images of old St. Nick to change into red and pink hearts on banners proclaiming, "I love you."

The assigned seats for each resident have changed, and now Betty needs help being fed and her cherry red lipstick is smeared all over her face.

Why does such decline happen to us? Why can't we all just live forever? I wonder if they are aware of everything that is happening around them.

Dinner conversations are always changing, although they always focus on the past. I don't believe most of the residents remember what happened the day before. They seem to talk mostly about childhood memories, high school accomplishments, or work they did on the farm or in the office. The one thing they never talk about is the reason why they ended up in here.

Each resident has a different nutrition list, stuff that they can and cannot eat. Garry has a hard time swallowing, so his food is served purée. Elizabeth is able to have solid food... for the moment. When I help with feeding, I usually end up helping the same two residents. Both are mute, so they share their appreciation through warm smiles and head nods.

This one lady I'll never forget, always gets mad at me for having "long hair" and "red boots". She used to be a head-mistress at a girls' finishing school. She thinks these two attributes to be the most terrible, and luckily I have both.

You are probably wondering, at this point, why I take time out of my day to come here if they will not even remember me in a few hours. I always remember them, and I always will. I remember the good days when each and every resident has seemed calm and happy, the bad ones when no one can seem to get them to relax, and the days that drag on for so long that I feel like my volunteer status will turn into me joining here as a resident myself.

I pass by Betty's old room, and there is a new name I do not recognise along with new furniture and a different colour scheme than Betty's. Another change. What kind of stories does the new resident have to tell? Maybe some about her greatest accomplishments. As I make eye contact with her, she smiles at me. I stand still for a second, attempting to take the newness in. I finally come to my senses and smile back.

"Hi, Louise, I'm Dakota! It's nice to meet you!"

"Hello, dear. I seem to have misplaced my book. Do you mind helping me find it?"

As I swallow down the lump in my throat, I proceed to help her find her book, one she tells me her son bought for her as a Christmas gift. She also tells me how her son is a doctor, a brilliant surgeon for that matter. I think I could start to like Louise. Even is she isn't Betty.

As days go by, the flowers bloom, the leaves change their colour, the people grow older, their smiles appear and eventually fade away, but the one thing that never changes about this place is the wealth of love that makes it feel like home.

June

Rachel Martino

When I was nine my family and I packed up and moved to Guelph. This meant a new house, a new neighbourhood, and to my absolute horror, a new school. On my first day at JRH Elementary, I sat on the bus next to a girl in a pink furry sweater, Hannah Montana jeans, and pink and black punk glasses. I said "Hey." She puked all over me.

This was how I met June. We waited in the office together, smelling of puke, for our parents to bring us new clothes. We bonded over our mutual love for Children's Place and Family Channel. We talked about our pets, her dog Snuggles, my cat General Fluffers. We then moved on to the twins sitting in the back of the bus who were very cute. Of course, we didn't really know what this meant, but TV and *Tiger Beat* magazine had told us that anyone with a straight nose, high cheekbones, and large eyes was cute, and so they were. We even had birthdays in the same month, and immediately began thinking of joint birthday parties. It felt perfect, like it was meant to be. By the time we walked to our class in clean clothes, we weren't nervous anymore.

Throughout that first year, we faced some troubles as every famous duo does at some point or another. We even defeated our arch nemesis, Ashley Parker Jameson. According to us, she was the devil incarnate, attempting to split us up. In reality, she was just a girl trying to make friends, and we definitely weren't the heroes in her story. By the end of the year, she had transferred to a new school. We were very proud of ourselves.

June and I were inseparable after that. When we got to middle school and were supposed to be in different classes, June's Mom made the school administration swap her into my mine.

That year was one of our best. We had a great teacher who always let us pick our groups and seating plans, which meant that we were never separated. This was how we got to May of our seventh grade year – and the problem.

That week was different. June was leaving for Vancouver for seven days. It was the longest we had been apart since that first meeting. Even during the summers, we would rotate who hosted the weekly Friday night sleepover. I was terrified of being alone, I had never had to do it before. I would have to endure five full days of school without June. Where would I sit at lunch? Who would I do projects with? Would the Y-Splitter that we used to listen to music together in class have no purpose for an ENTIRE week? These questions plagued me all Sunday night. Luckily this meant that by Monday morning I was far too "sick" to go to school, staying home for the whole day instead. Unfortunately, this only delayed the inevitable. By the time Tuesday came around I was forced to go to school, my parents no longer believing my terrible acting skills.

School was lonely for the morning. By the afternoon we were starting a new project, a group project. I was bursting out of my skin, I was so nervous. I eventually got partnered up with a girl named Heather. In my mind, Heather was a pixie. A very energetic pixie. She used to run around the square out front of our school while waiting for the bus, screaming the whole time. We bonded immediately. Her two friends, Sally and Michelle, were often partnered up and she permanently felt like the third wheel, so having me around was a huge relief. We spent the week together and by the time it was over we were friends. Sally and I would pull all-nighters, playing Crazy Eight Countdown over Facetime and gossiping about everyone we knew. Michelle was one of the busiest people that I had ever met. She excelled at handling stress. The four of us together felt complete. Heather was always excited, Sally and I would gossip, and Michelle was our peace-keeper. It was like a Family Channel show come true.

That week was amazing. Instead of being nervous about what would happen if June was gone, I was nervous about what would happen when she came back. June and I were like Bert and Ernie. We didn't need the rest of Sesame Street before, just each other. Now that I had met other people and liked them, I was scared that I was going to have give them up, or give June up. I wasn't overly interested in either of these options. I wanted the best of both worlds. I had never had to deal with any sort of conflict among friends, so I thought that there wouldn't be any problems merging my two friend groups. Whoops.

When June came back my other friends began to back off. I didn't understand what I had done wrong. Suddenly, with June back, it was like she had never left. Like the last week had never happened. Eventually I confronted Sally about it.

"I didn't want June to feel completely ditched. She's just not my kind of person you know? There's nothing bad about it but," she whispered this part to me, "she's kinda weird."

Sally acted like this was some big secret. She even followed it up with a "but don't tell anyone I said that." What I didn't understand was how someone could like me but not June. I tried to explain to her, telling her that we were a package deal, and that once she got to know June she would really like her. I didn't tell her that June didn't like Sally, and that she thought that Sally was boring and unoriginal. Who could that have possibly helped? Definitely not me.

After a couple of weeks Sally came around to the idea and

invited us both to her upcoming birthday party. It was great. There was food, lots of people, everyone was on their phones playing the latest game. June didn't think it was so great. She didn't have a phone, and she was not such a huge fan of people, but I was too lost in my own bubble to see that. Sally kept inviting us to these events, and I kept going. June always had a reason why she couldn't come, be it ballet, or choir, or baby-sitting her sister. Maybe sometimes she really was busy, maybe sometimes she really wasn't. We would still hang out, but it wasn't the same. Eventually, I would go and hang out with Sally, Heather, and Michelle, leaving June alone. She said she was fine with it. I found out later that she wasn't.

We drifted apart, and by the time we started high school we still claimed to be best friends, but we weren't, at least not in the way that I had learned the word, not in the way that June had taught it to me. By the end of high school we were close to being complete strangers, just the distant string of memory tying us together. Those years of outdoor movie viewings, and sneaking out of her house to go into the forest at night and completely freak ourselves out were long gone, only a distant memory. We hadn't had a single class together for four years. I later learned that her Mom had gone into the guidance office and requested this, apparently she wanted her daughter to make new friends.

We met again years later. We were both in the final year of our undergrads, and she was visiting my university for a tour of a master's program. We met in a cafe that was a fusion between something and a bakery. She ordered fish-cookie-tacos, and I ordered the deep-fried-mango-cookie. We talked about SnapChat, school, and Netflix. It was our twenty-one year old version of talking about Children's place and Family Channel.

She texted me later that day. Apparently she got food poisoning. We had come full circle.

Midtown Road

Camille Smiderle

My eyes fluttered open and met the glaring light of the mid-day sun. I noticed dirt clinging to my arm as I checked my watch. The palms of my hands were bleeding. It was 12:30. I was laying on a dirt road with a name I didn't recognise. "Mid-town Road", the sign above me said. The gravel and earth beneath me were wet and warm and I could feel my t-shirt stuck to my back. Not a single person was in sight. My bike laid bent at its middle next to me, it's crinkled wheels spinning ever so slightly. My head pounded in a steady rhythm, each beat as searing as the last. My body felt lined with lead as I cautiously sat up.

Around me were fields – brown with patches of green. It was probably corn, I thought to myself. I sat up, slowly, trying to figure out where I was. Last I remembered, I was riding my bike on a country road on the outskirts of the city, and this didn't look too far off. My muscles tensed as I shakily stood up, looked down at my acid wash jeans and dusted them off. As I dipped my head to clean off my knees I felt a sting of pain different than the one I'd woken up to. I placed my fingers in my hair and quickly found a large bump. I must've fallen off my bike, I told myself.

I didn't see any point in standing around, so I parted with my bike and started to walk in the hope of finding someone who would let me borrow their phone. After about an hour of walking under the sun's merciless glare, I noticed something odd. The fields looked the same, the sky looked the same, it all looked the same. There didn't seem to be a single difference in landscape. Of course it all looks the same, you're in the middle of corn field nowhere. Keep walking, I thought.

* * * * *

The sun stayed hung in the middle of the sky and the heat had become more bearable as a breeze made itself at home in the landscape. I was still walking. Everything was still the same. As I walked, I spotted something in the distance, it was a road sign. Thank God, I have to be getting somewhere, I thought. My eyes squinted as I zeroed in on the sign with a laser focus. As I did, I saw something. I'd heard of mirages before, or how heat can change how you see objects in the distance, but this was different. This, looked like a computer glitch. I rubbed my eyes, thinking the heat had gotten to me after all. When I opened them and looked in a different direction, there it was again. In a single second the cornfield went from a cohesive blend of green and yellow to a mosaic filled in with what looked like white lights. Before I knew it, I was at the road sign. It said "Midtown Road".

I stood under the sign and tried to make sense of what I was seeing. Midtown Road. No North or West, no East or South. Just, Midtown Road. I was so wrapped up in thought I almost didn't hear the soft spoken, "Excuse me," emerge from just over my shoulder. I whipped around and my eyes met those of a young, blonde woman. She was dressed in khaki shorts, hiking boots and a thin blue t-shirt. Scrapes covered her knees and she was cradling her arm. It looked limp. She shuffled backwards as I looked at her.

Her green eyes spoke of desperation and fear. "I – I'm so sorry to bother you, but I haven't seen anyone for hours and I don't know where I am and I think my arm's broken…" Tears started to inch down her face. "I – I'm Serina, by the way." I scanned her for a moment then relaxed my shoulders.

"I'm Laura, sorry for scaring you. I don't know where we are either. I've been walking for hours looking for someone. You're the first person I've seen. What happened?" I said, gesturing to her arm.

"I wish I knew. I was walking beside the fields and heard someone scream. I ran in and woke up with this." She glanced at her arm.

"How long have you been walking?"

"Uh, it, it had to have been at least an hour, but I can't be sure." She looked up towards the sky as she spoke. A few moments passed.

"Can I ask you something?" I said, looking up at the girl in front of me.

"Oh, sure go ahead." Her eyes were moving between the landscape and myself.

"I know this might make me sound crazy, but does everything sort of look… exactly the same to you?" I gestured to the air around me.

"I mean, I – I guess so, but –"

"And have you noticed the road signs are all the same?"

"Well sure, but some roads are just really –"

"And the sun hasn't moved at all!" I yelled.

"I – I'm sorry," Serina said.

Exasperated, I kicked the road sign. When I turned back around I noticed the tension in my new travel companion's face had grown. I saw the fingers of her limp arm ever so slightly reach out to me as her overall stance started to stiffen.

"Maybe we should turn around and try the other way?"

I didn't reply. My frustration grew along with the silence between us, and I turned away to put my head in my hands, but was interrupted by what felt like a soft wall meeting my forehead. Startled, I stumbled backwards and looked ahead of me. There was nothing there. All that laid in front of me were blue skies, the dirt road and the corn fields. I took a step forwards and the tips of my toes met with the same rejection as before.

"C'mon, let's just try the other way," Serina said behind me. "I think I might have seen a building back there. Laura, let's go," she urged, as I patted down the invisible wall. "Let's GO!"

I felt her hand grip my shoulder tightly and pull me towards her. I grabbed it and turned around. The hand belonged to the arm she'd been cradling, and it was no longer limp. I looked her in the eye. Any trace of fear or vulnerability was gone. Her face was hardened and poised. We stood in a dead stare, neither of us moved.

"Your arm clearly isn't broken. What's going on here?" I asked, still locking her wrist in my hand.

Her face remained expressionless. "I just think we should go the other way. So let's go." She calmly exhaled. I let go of her wrist, scoffed and turned to face the invisible wall. The moment I turned my back I heard the glide of metal being freed from an enclosure. "I'll say this one more time. Turn around and walk the other way."

I turned to see Serina facing me with a long handled knife. Without a second thought I ducked and kicked her knees with all of the remaining strength I had. I sent her backwards and her head slammed against the ground.

I leaped towards the knife that left her hand during the fall and turned back to the wall. I felt for the barrier then stuck the knife through a space as high as I could reach and raked it down to the ground. I put my hands on either side of the separation and ripped it open. Light flooded my sight and I blindly pushed myself through the opening. When my eyes adjusted I met the stares of a dozen men and women in lab coats.

"Congratulations Laura, you survived."

GRADES 9 - 10

Strawberries

Jessica Stokes

Close your eyes, I command myself. Take a deep breath, count down from ten. I follow my own orders. I hate it down here, but I hate it when we are above ground as well. To be honest, I hate it here no matter the time of day, month, season, or whether we are on the front lines or not. Then again, everyone would hate being in hell. The only consolation is that I know the Triple Entente have it worse. The thick Brits dug their trenches in a rush, and rumour says they did it horribly as well. So whoever is occupying them is living in a hell slightly more awful than ours. We, however, dug ours the way we do everything, properly and perfectly. Just like everything else we Germans complete. I reach ten and I reopen my eyes. The familiar dugout greets me, and the unpleasant noises return to my ears. One other good thing is that the bombs are not dropping at the same rate my heart is beating. "Always looks at the glasses as half full," my mother would tell me.

I would always respond the same way: "But if I look at them half empty then I am either right or pleasantly surprised." Here in the Somme there are no glasses to be half full or half empty. So whichever is true doesn't matter.

"Oi! Friedrich!" says Wilhelm who is laying on the bunk above me. Then he lowers his voice to a whisper. "What are you thinking about?" Wilhelm likes to make conversation during times like these. He finds it calming.

I pause considering my answer. Even though I am bitter, upsetting Wilhelm would not help either of us. "The best kind of fruit," I say to him.

This catches his interest. He appears to perk up a little. "How are you judging the fruit, by flavour, amount of preparation needed, size, or value?" he asks, moving from his bunk to mine. I sit up and swing my legs down to make room for my blond-haired, blue-eyed friend. I occasionally chuckle at how different we are; his hair is very blond and straight, the absolute opposite from my black and curly mess.

"Would it be too complicated for you if I included all of these factors?" I question.

Hurt flickers across his face before he recognises my tease. "Not at all, for I have the answer," he says. I look at him in disbelief. "Watermelon," he says like it's a matter of fact.

I shake my head, indicating that he is incorrect.

"Why not? It's big, tastes nice. It's expensive. but all you have to do is cut it in half. Then it's ready to eat," he says.

"It's messy, it only tastes good in the summer, and it's made mostly of water," I reply.

Wilhelm murmurs something about how messiness has nothing to do with the greatness of a fruit. "What's your idea then?" he asks.

Once again I pause, thinking about my answer. "Oranges," I say. "Little mess, refreshing, easy to prepare."

This time Wilhelm shakes his head. "They have little mess because there is little substance to create mess," he says. "Bad value for money. Pick a different one." This continues for a while. I keep a mental tally of what we rule out and why.

Grapefruit: too sour without sugar and therefore too hard to prepare.

Grapes: too small.

Apples: can be expensive and if apples are the best, what kind of apple?

Raspberries: strange texture.

We take a break, each of us thinking about what really is the best fruit. We sit in silence and something surprises me. "Hey, did you hear that?" I look towards the entrance and he follows my gaze.

"No I didn't. What did you hear?" he questions. I look at him almost excited.

"Exactly what you heard. Nothing," I say. He looks confused for a second and then it clicks.

"The bombs have stopped," he says in awe. Then, as if on cue, in runs our commander.

"Everyone up and to your posts!" he shouts, and everyone who could have been asleep wakes abruptly and starts to get ready. "Prepare for an infantry attack!"

He leaves and runs to his post. I jump up and tie my boots tight. I grab my coat and start to make my way to the machine guns. Wilhelm is behind me. After all, I would be very inefficient without him loading the gun. We're ready in record time. But there is no one coming. I can see almost all of no man's land. It is a barren wasteland in every sense of the word. Not even trees are here, and neither are the French.

"This makes no sense," I say, "Where are the little vermin?" I turn to Wilhelm who is also focusing on no man's land. At least eight minutes must have passed since the artillery attack halted.

"Strawberries." He replies so quietly I almost didn't hear him.

I frown. "This is not the time," I say.

"Yes it is. I want the answer," he snaps.

"Seriously, Wilhelm, not now," I whisper unhappily.

"Stop talking to me like I'm five years old." His anger comes without warning.

I turn my head to look at him. "What are you on about?" I ask.

"I am on about that strawberries are the best fruit," he says firmly.

"They are not," I say. Why can he not be reasoned with?

"They are," he replies.

"You're wrong," I tell him

"I am correct," he says.

I open my mouth to tell him to stop being immature but I am interrupted.

"FIRE!" shouts a commander. I turn my head to no man's land. It is occupied by the French coming over their trench with rifles in hand. I pull the trigger and keep my head low.

Have you ever tried to explain a complicated maths problem to someone younger than yourself? They just don't understand, and the harder you try the more you fail, so you give in anyway and move on. Or have you ever had a really bad cough that makes your voice hoarse and whenever you have to answer a question the sound of your voice is really horrible to listen to? Your voice sounds so strange that people just laugh at you so you have to talk over their noise, but the more you talk the more they laugh and the more your throat hurts? It's an endless circle. Trying to explain what the land looks like right now is like those situations. Except you can tell that the other person just doesn't see what you see. They don't see the magnitude of wasted blood. They just don't understand.

Wilhelm grabs my elbow and I turn to him. He's sitting down breathing heavily. There is a tear in his sleeve on his right shoulder. A tear that travels through his skin as well. Wilhelm has been shot. I don't know how or why but it's happened. I kneel down trying to think of what to do. What do I do? How do I stop the bleeding?

"You should calm down a bit first," he says. I was unaware I was speaking out loud. I take a deep breath. The shock must be keeping him calm. I take out my knife and cut a thin strand of cloth from the end of my shirt.

"I'll wrap your shoulder in this and get someone to take you to a doctor," I tell him. He nods and I work quickly.

"Why?" he asks.

"Why what?" I say meeting his gaze.

"You never said why strawberries are not the best."

I open my mouth ready to say a million things. A million things as to why they are not the best or why this is not the time for a debate or why this really isn't important right now. Instead I reply simply and seriously, "Because strawberry juice looks like blood."

I shout for assistance, and eventually someone comes to pull him up and wrap his good arm around their shoulder to share his weight.

Wilhelm remains silent and so do I. I think I understand why he was angry. The thought of others people's blood is infuriating to me. I don't understand why. This war is taking a toll on everyone, no matter who you are, where you come from, or which side of no man's land you live on. I'm informed that his injury is not fatal and to wait for a new companion. I follow my orders and keep my helmet on and my head down. Never again will I eat a strawberry, I think to myself. Because never again do I want to see blood. A younger looking boy comes to my gun to aid me. I reposition myself and pull the trigger.

2nd PLACE

Into Focus

Holly Lavergne

Lyla tossed her bulging backpack onto the floor and collapsed in a heap on her bed. She thought about escaping into sleep, but quickly shook herself awake and began compiling a list of the numerous things she had to accomplish: finish chemistry project, study for math test, start essay outline, read history package, take shower. How was she ever going to do everything? Did teachers have nothing better to do than hand out heaps of work? She loathed them all.

Enmity tumbled from her, a constant stream of worries filling her thoughts and speech. She just didn't care.

Lyla got up and grabbed her water bottle, taking a drink as she got ready for the long night, just like the many long nights before it. She got out her textbooks and pencil case, tossing them carelessly on her desk. Then she sat down and began to work, hunched within her own tense sphere of panic, lost within her self-created world, her fabricated reality. Slowly, sentences grew to paragraphs, and stacks of papers rose like buildings in the skyline of her effable city.

Suddenly, just above her frantic scrawling, an envelope slid anomalously off her shelf. A dozen photos fell out, scattering across her desk. She groaned and pushed through her metropolis of words, grabbing at the pieces of glossy paper. Her friend Amber had given her these useless old pictures for her birthday; now they were just cluttering her workspace.

As she gathered them up, she glanced down at the photo on top, a seemingly innocent rectangle encasing the faces of two girls outside on a hot summer's day, with paint and glitter splattered everywhere. Lyla remembered that day. She and Amber were maybe six years old and they had been making props for their play. They got a bit crazy with the colours, and by the end, even their shadows were tinted with wisps of ink.

As her fingers brushed the corner of the last photo, Lyla felt the wind knocked out of her. She heard the echoes of high pitched laughter, and her vision cleared to see the glittering faces of two young girls, colour painted across their clothes like wind. She gasped and dropped the photo, lyrical voices composing her thoughts as they spiralled through her mind.

What had just happened?

She shook her head. Life's not fair, giving you moments like that only to snatch them away and reward you with piles of endless work and stress. The voices had disappeared from her thoughts, replaced by the usual stream of loathing. She was never going to have a day like that again, with no worries or responsibilities. She would never be free.

Lyla picked up her pen, getting back to work, when another photo caught her eye. She and Amber were standing at the top of a mountain with a bright blue lake and picturesque town sprawling behind them. Their arms were raised and the sun illuminated their freckled faces. Lyla hesitated to pick up the photo, unsure of what was to come. She reached for it anyway.

Once again, she felt a whirlwind of space and light and memory, as the sight of another world and the thoughts of her mother echoed in a voice she usually tried to ignore:

I watch my daughter Lyla and her friend Amber rush to look at the view. It's stunning, especially after our long hike. Lyla's face breaks into a wide smile as she and Amber begin to jump up and down. Totally worth it.

"Girls, turn around. Say cheese!" I snap a photo of them, with their hands waving in the air. Lyla turns to Amber to whisper something and they fall over laughing. The world is out there, just waiting for them to explore it. I hope they stay like this forever.

Lyla is there, years ago on their vacation to the mountains. She watches herself, sees her complete awe as she looks at the horizon of endless peaks, dotted with burgundy thatched roofs. She remembers thinking that the world is amazing – remembers repeating that she will never forget that moment, the laughing and smiling friendship she had formed.

I hope they stay like this forever.

She blinks and her senses are engulfed like a cascading river at twilight. Her vision goes dark as she tumbles into reality. But which reality?

Lyla opens her eyes. She looks from the pile of papers to the envelope. She hesitantly reaches for another photo, this one a selfie. Amber and she were at the mall last October, but she doesn't even remember taking the photo. She touches the picture and is instantly tossed into a new landscape, with Amber's voice searching her mind:

I look over at Lyla as we walk through the mall. I love walking around and looking at stuff! It's so much fun to make jokes with friends and then laugh. And then next week and next year we'll remember that thing and it'll still be hilarious. That's what I love about life. There's always something amazing.

"So d'you wanna go to the bookstore?" I ask. Lyla groans and says she doesn't like books – that they're all pretty much the same. I say, "Oh," and then we decide to go look at clothes.

"Let's take a selfie," I say. "To remember." I take out my phone and smile, but Lyla just raises the corners of her mouth and grimaces. I wish Lyla would enjoy everything more. In fact, all she does now is complain. And maybe I'm the only one still laughing at our jokes. Are they our jokes? Or just mine?

I turn to look at Amber. We stand together in the mall, but we look so starkly different. Two girls, one hunched with eyebrows raised and one with a glowing smile illuminating her face. What's the difference? I guess… well… Amber still cares. She cares about everything, and I… I just worry about marks. All I did that day was complain about my math test. Since then, I can hardly remember anything, apart from sitting alone at my desk.

Are they our jokes? Or just mine?

This time, I seem to float back to my bedroom. I look down at myself: my clothes, my room, my stuff, my everything. How did this happen? I pick up the other photos, looking through them one by one and laughing out loud. I see a note inside the envelope: it's a sketch of a giraffe in a bikini, from that summer camp with the grape juice song. I want them to be our jokes again.

I pin the pictures on my corkboard and stuff my papers in my backpack, along with all my schoolwork. That's not my only reality. In fact, I never have to go there again. I can create new realities.

I pick up my phone and send a text. Not, "Did you get the math questions?" or "Can you send me a picture of the biology note?" I haven't typed these words together in years.

"Want to go to the bookstore tomorrow?"

And my reality rises like mountains on the horizon of my ineffable adventure.

A Forget-Me-Not Sky

Crystal Lu

We always told ourselves that our friendship would last forever.

That was before we realised that the world wasn't as simple as we had thought.

The sun shone brilliantly across the ripe blue sky; there wasn't a single cloud in sight. The grass sparkled like a sea of glass. Its light rippled across our paved driveway. I remember wearing orange that spring day.

I was waiting for you on our back deck. It was very peaceful there. The birds chattered soothingly as I ran my fingers across a small patch of the deck's chipped paint.

When you arrived, I quickly ran up to you. My bare feet flew through the dirt and grass, smudging earth between my toes.

I smiled, breathless. I wore the grin of a child: bright, naive, and unassuming. I was still a kid back then. You didn't smile back.

Before I could say anything, I heard you sigh. It was heavy and full of melancholy.

At the time, I didn't realise that your mannerisms indicated that you were sad. To me, sadness meant tears. There was another layer of emotion that I had yet to discover. You had always been a little precocious.

But, I could tell that something was wrong. The glimmer that you always had in your eye was gone. You reminded me of a candle that had been snuffed out.

I reached to pat your shoulder, but you flinched and jerked back. You didn't look angry, but something that resembled pain flashed across your face.

I remember how fiercely you stared at me. Your brown eyes seemed so unreadable, until I reflected on this memory years later.

Everything else happened so quickly.

I remember how you retracted your hands from your pockets with caution. Then, you shoved a fistful of flowers at me. They had been crushed a little, but they were still beautiful. I remember being captivated by their unusual colour.

You told me that they were forget-me-nots. You explained that this was a goodbye present. Your mother had received a new job that was far away from here. You told me that you were moving, and that it was unlikely that we'd be able to see each other as often.

I was a little shocked at the sudden goodbye. I had known you since we were in diapers. We did everything together. You knew me better than I did.

I shook my head.

After a moment of silence, I spoke up.

I said that no matter what, we'd always be best friends. I told you that nothing could separate us; not distance, not time. I believed it, too. Maybe it was a little foolish of me.

Your features lifted into a smile. Yet there was something estranged about your smile. It seemed foreign, as if we had already begun drifting apart.

You waved goodbye and went on your way.

A single blue petal fell away from your gift.

As the weeks passed, we did a decent job of keeping in touch. I called you a couple of times a week. You seemed to be doing well.

I was quite lonely. I didn't realise it until you left, but I didn't have very many friends. I never needed anyone else because I always had you.

Our friendship was like bright paint in a plain room. Now that it was gone, the room felt quite bare and hollow. Empty and dark.

Your absence soon became a bigger hole in my life. I remember hearing a funny joke, and turning to tell you when I remembered that you were no longer by my side.

Sometimes I wondered what your opinion would be on a certain subject until I realised that you were gone.

Sometimes I stared at the flowers you gave me and hoped that you would magically come back. However, the hope I once held so strongly soon faded away. After awhile, I grew tired. My heart felt like lead. I had now become accustomed to that heavy sadness.

I knew it stemmed from staying in the past rather than living in the present, but there was so much happiness that I couldn't let go of. I was scared that if I did, I would forget everything.

Forget everything we've been through.

Forget us.

Forget you.

I grew to realise that some things are out of our control, and that there was nothing we could do. And as the months past, the phone calls dwindled.

And dwindled.

Until there were none.

By then a couple of years had passed. My heart had healed over.

The forget-me-nots had finally withered away.

It was a wonder that those flowers lasted so long, but looking back on them, I realise that friendship is similar to flowers.

If you don't tend to a flower, give it love and care, it will not flourish. If you leave it for too long, it could wither away and disappear.

But some flowers can weather storms and come back even stronger.

Unlike the forget-me-nots, I eventually forgot. I learned to focus on the present, and only occasionally to look back. I now had a wonderful group of friends, had received my first job, and had learned how to drive. I had changed so much in a few short years.

When I did look back, you, someone I cared deeply for as a child, were just a blur. I could barely remember your eyes, or even the role you played in my life. You remained an untouchable memory.

It was my second year of university. I had stayed in my hometown and had decided to study journalism.

It was one of those sunny but cold days right after all the snow has melted. The breeze bit into my skin and bones. I shivered, and tightened my scarf. I was downtown.

As I turned the corner, my hat caught the wind and floated away in the opposite direction. I panicked a bit, and chased it after it, derailing me from my previous course.

I finally caught up to it a couple of streets later when it got stuck in a tree. I gingerly tugged my hat out from within the branches, and stuffed it in my bag. I didn't want to do anymore running today.

I stopped and glanced at my surroundings. Everything seemed mostly familiar, but I never really spent time in this part of downtown. As I caught my breath, I stared at the sky and contemplated my next course of action.

The sky struck me as comforting and bright. Its colour felt familiar, although I was not quite sure why.

When another gust of wind raked against my flesh, I decided to enter the cafe that was right nearby. I figured I could still get some work done here. I wasn't about to run a couple of hundred meters just to get to my regular cafe.

As I stepped into the building, I bumped into someone heading out.

My eyes met theirs as I began muttering an apology.

Midway, I fell silent.

Their brown eyes did not leave mine.

"Is that you…?"

And then I realised.

The colour of the sky…

…was the colour of forget-me-nots.

The Little Girl in the Back of the Crowd

Jess Ridley

The silence fills the crowd. The whole auditorium. The music stops, the spotlight, blinding me, burning my eyes, making my skin hot, reflecting, off of my crown and dazzling white tutu, shining onto the stage.

The music begins. I see the male dancer, Jason, I think his name is, in my peripheral vision. I don't know him that well, but I have faith in him. He goes along with the choreography, and by the end of it, we've completed the dance with perfect accuracy.

The crowd goes wild. Cheering for our dance. That sound. The sound of the applause, that feeling when I catch sight of the little girl in the back row of the balcony who saw me dance, and wants to be just like me. That moment when I become her idol, and flash back to when I was her. That moment when she becomes a dancer too, and I see her up on stage, and I smile.

We take our bow, then exit stage left. However, Jason's grip fumbles on my hand, and I tip over my point shoes, twisting my ankle. The audience giggles.

Tears filling my eyes, I run into my mother's arms, standing there in her backstage crew uniform and black headset, arms wide open, and cry into her shoulder. She strokes my hair and holds me in her cool embrace. "There, there. It's okay. It's not your fault."

I look up at her cloudy green eyes, filled with love. "You're right," I say. I whip around and turn to my partner, pointing my finger inches away from his face. He leans back in fear. "It's his fault!" I scream.

My mom places her hands on my shoulders. "Exactly. You did everything right. He's the one who made a mistake." She shoots him a death glare, and his eyes go wide. We watch him run off to the hallway, totally panicked.

I turn back to my mom, smiling. "Now, let's get some ice on that ankle," she says, sitting me down beside the curtain. "Hey, Mark? Yeah, we need some ice back here," she says into her headset. A few minutes later, a man comes backstage with the ice, with which mom takes great care to wrap it around my ankle.

But all of it stops dead in its tracks when she comes in. The air becomes cold and still, as everyone, parents, coaches, contestants, stare at her. As the door to the hallway opens, the light from the hallway floods the dark corners backstage. Everyone looks to the door, and we all see the silhouette of a slender young girl standing in the doorway.

When she steps through the doorway, I feel strange. Confused. I can usually read people well. A girl controlled by a stage mom or a free spirit... but I can't read her. She's dressed like she's still rehearsing – a knee-length flowing black skirt and a black bodice, both completely plain and undecorated. Most dancers, including me, have their hair in a dancer's bun, but her long hair is flowing freely.

I lean over to the boy beside me. "Who's that?" I ask.

"She's a newcomer. Jaquelyn Theodore. No one knows where she came from, but the second she appeared onstage, people started raving about her dance style," he says.

"What's her style?"

"She performs like it's just another rehearsal. Never gets into an actual costume, never takes a bow. She's even gone on record saying she's never tried her best before. She's never pushed herself in her life, but she has so much natural talent that she wins anyway. And it's not like she's the smug type either. She's so quiet," he explains.

We look so different. Me, with my gaudy, bedazzled, white tutu, and my dancer's bun, and her with her totally black rehearsal outfit, and long, freely flowing black hair. We look like yin and yang.

A crew member opens the curtains, as I peer around his blackened figure to watch this sudden miracle of dance.

That's when I see it and my jaw drops. She's standing perfectly on point, but she's not wearing point shoes. In fact, she's not wearing any shoes. She's completely barefoot.

"She cannot be taking this seriously," I whisper to the boy. "Newbies know nothing. She's going to be a one-hit wonder all her life."

The boy ignores me, completely entranced by her opening pose. I'll admit, as competitive and confident as I am, that opening pose of hers, with one arm raised above her head, looks striking. So graceful, but not elegant. She looks... natural. It's strange.

Every other newbie I've seen is like me. A crazed workaholic with the gaudiest, glitteriest tutu. That's what I've always associated with the word elegant.

This girl is not elegant. She's beautiful. I wish I could read her. I wish, I wish, I wish so badly that I could see what's behind that long hair and black costume. I want to see her motivations, her dreams, her goals.

The music begins. It's one of my least favourite pieces. So bland, so generic... so easy. Theme to *Swan Lake*. Every year I have to hear this. Everyone uses it. I roll my eyes. Hopefully this style of hers is worth it.

She starts to dance. Her movements are slow and graceful, her long hair trailing behind her. The boy beside me is right.

She really isn't trying. She's the single best dancer that I've ever seen. In fact, I feel intimidated by her talent, but I know I'm not alone when I see that she really doesn't care about this dance. She's probably wondering what she's going to do this weekend. What kind of newcomer is she? What kind of person is she?

Then everything changes when she goes into the spins. Her eyes meet mine, and they go wide. Instantly, she stops dancing, and stares at me. The music stops along with her. Whispers and mumbles come up in the crowd. I can't believe what's going on. No one, newbie or otherwise, stops mid-number. More importantly, why is she staring at me?

Our eyes are locked. I'm looking into her eyes, but I still can't read her. Have we met? Has she seen me perform before?

"Has this happened before?" I whisper to the boy beside me.

"No! I saw her first two performances, and she placed gold at both sectionals and regionals. You'd think she'd take nationals more seriously, even if she isn't trying her best," the boy whispers back.

Suddenly, the music returns, and she begins to dance once more, taking it from the beginning. Except this time, it's different. There's so much more energy, more passion, even more grace. I look closer. She's... smiling? She's changed. She cares about the dance. In fact, she loves it. She's happy.

I just... can't understand. What happened? This girl was bored and uninterested until she locked eyes with me. When her dance is done, the crowd goes wild. She's not going to win, because she stopped mid-dance, but the audience loves her more than any other routine that's been up today. She's the strangest newbie I've ever seen. Why does she only actually try now?

She walks backstage, ignoring all the stares, and comes

over to me. She crouches down next to me. She smiles, then mouths, "Thank you." I see it. Finally, I can read her.

I've made my way to the top through desperate training. I was a perfect dancer, a perfect balance. This girl on the other hand, she came to the top through hard work, yes, but also through luck, and sheer talent. She wouldn't truly try her best until she finally met the one who inspired her to dance.

She's the little girl in the back of the crowd. The little girl who did a cute little routine for her grandparents in a princess dress. The little girl who saw the ballet with her parents, and who saw her soon-to-be idol up on stage, glittering in her tutu. The one who decided on that day that she would be a world famous ballerina.

The dancer she saw that day was me. It made sense now. Maybe she wasn't a little girl at the time, but deep in my bones, I feel it. Both of our dreams have come true. She's danced her way to her idol, and in her own way, at that, and I... I've finally inspired the girl in the back of the crowd.

And someday, she will too.

Assassin

Naomi Boisvert

Darnell sat quite still on the cold bench, clutching an old, worn notebook on his lap. He fiddled with the bright green bookmark nervously, brushing his violently purple hair to the side. This was his first solo job. He kept repeating the name in his mind: Alan Gordan. The man should be at the bus stop that night on his way home from the bar.

Darnell tightened his grip on the notebook. It was getting late now. The target would miss his bus if he didn't show up in the next half hour, and Darnell would have to go home. A shiver ran up his spine at the thought of reporting a failed job to his family. His mother, father, and sisters had all done many jobs before this one, and they all had advice for him. They had told him not to show any fear, to surprise the target.

Darnell was pulled from his thoughts at the sight of a man walking toward the bus stop. He was tall, probably six feet at least, and well muscled. Darnell couldn't help thinking that he was handsome, and inwardly hoped that he wasn't Gordan. The man sat down beside him.

"What bus are you taking, kid?" He had a nice voice.

"I – I'm not taking a bus," Darnell stuttered. "I'm just waiting for my father."

"Does he have dyed hair too? Not to be rude, but I don't think purple hair is natural."

Darnell laughed at that, and replied, "He must have dyed his hair then, because blue isn't a natural hair colour either."

The man laughed. It was booming and rough, like a dog barking. "You might be right, kid."

They sat in silence for a moment before the stranger spoke again. "So what's your name, kid? I'll tell you mine if you tell me yours."

Darnell was quiet, worried that the man wouldn't talk to him if he knew his last name. The Ramore family was infamous in this town, after all. "I'm Darnell." Fortunately the stranger didn't press for his last name.

"My name's Alan. Alan Gordan."

Darnell froze. His terror must have shown on his face, because Alan suddenly looked concerned. "What's wrong, Darnell? I won't judge, you can tell me."

Darnell turned to Alan. "Do you know the Ramore family?"

"Everyone knows about them, kiddo. Why?"

Darnell swallowed nervously. How was he going to tell Alan that he was sent after him?

"Come on kid," Alan said quietly, as if talking to a very upset child. "What's wrong? Is it because they're after me? I can leave if you don't feel safe around me."

"No! Don't leave!" Darnell was shouting. "I mean, I don't think you understand. It's not what you think."

"Then what's wrong?" Alan was getting visibly confused. "What else could it possibly be?"

Darnell decided just to tell him. "They sent me to k-kill you. They're my family." Darnell felt tears streaming down his face, and wondered when he had started crying. He looked up at Alan, who seemed to have gone into shock.

"Well," Alan started, "That's definitely not what I expected."

"You're not afraid?"

"Are you gonna do it?"

"No. I don't want to kill you, but if I don't –"

Alan interrupted. "Hold it right there, kid. You don't have to kill me. I can help you."

Darnell was stunned. "How?" Alan smiled kindly.

"I can get you a place to stay, or you can stay with me. I'm an expert at these things. How else would I have hid from your father for so long?"

"I've got a question for you, Alan."

"Shoot." Alan seemed to wince at his choice of words.

Darnell hesitated for a moment. "Why is my dad after you, anyway? Did you do something to him?"

Alan went quiet, and Darnell worried that he might have crossed a line until Alan answered. "It was quite a while ago, so I'm not sure if I remember it right. One night, around this time, I was walking home from work. When I walked past the old alley between the welding shop where I work and the garage, I heard screaming from inside. I was the only one still there at the time, so I ran into the alley to see what was happening. I only saw it for a moment, because I didn't want to be seen, but it was your father. He had just killed one of my co-workers, and he must have seen me before I ran, because he's still trying to kill me. I just wish I could have saved my coworker. He had three kids at the time."

Darnell didn't realise he was staring until after the story was finished. "Wow."

Alan laughed. "Yeah. It's quite the story, huh?"

They were silent for a while, and Darnell had his answer. "I'll come with you. I have nothing to lose anyway."

Alan grinned wolfishly. "So, if your parents weren't who they are, what would you do with your life? Any plans for when you're with me?"

Darnell smiled at that. "Well, I've always wanted to be a doctor. I'd much rather save people's lives than take them."

Alan smiled as the bus pulled up to the stop. The doors opened slowly, and a man stood in the doorway to get off the bus. Darnell's heart skipped a beat, and he dropped the notebook. The man in the doorway was his father.

GRADES 7 - 8

Strings

McKenna McFatridge

Rain poured and stung my blotchy, red face like acid with every drop; the sharp wind whipped around my hair and nipped at the sleeves of my loose jacket. Yet, I dragged on, continuing to carry myself through the cement jungle, past the Albion and Church of Our Lady and down by the Market Square. No one was outside in the mixture of bricks, cement and street lights that made up downtown Guelph. It was rare and rather puzzling to find it so empty, especially in the fall when the leaves were changing into bright, flamboyant flicks of fire at the end of every branch. But, then again, it was pouring rain and ten thirty in the morning, so perhaps it did make a fair amount of sense.

I turned a sharp corner and crossed the street, no traffic on either side, focusing on the poppies that had been solemnly painted onto the road, matching the one I had had embroidered onto his – my RCAF jacket. I felt my grip tighten on the case I was carrying as the wind continued its harsh pursuit, practically sniffing out that my ears weren't cold and purposely attacking them. It was then that I arrived at a decrepit looking red brick building, a small hole-in-the-wall place that was shoved between two much bigger ones like a long forgotten book, graffiti lining the small gaps along the two sides where the buildings met.

Taking a deep breath, I pushed open the old, oak door with one hand, the other wielding my case like some sort of makeshift weapon. A musty, familiar smell instantly hit my nose and I breathed in deeply, enjoying it as much as some people may when they beat a new level of a game. It was a triumphant smell, indicating I had pushed through the rain and finally, finally arrived. Behind the counter sat a middle aged man, who the years had clearly not been kind to. I had never seen him here before, he must've been new. His back was to a wall coated head to toe in ancient fix-me-up guitars and violins that looked like they had last been played in the 1800s. To anyone else, this would've been an instant turn off but, for me, it indicated the value of this place – the only place I would trust enough to accomplish what I needed done without completely ruining the instrument.

The man at the counter looked up and smiled, his eyes squinting for a moment before laughing and waving me over. Still soaking wet, I tried my best to avoid the books that had toppled over on the floor and the cases that had been lazily dumped aside them. I set my own case carefully down on the counter as he narrowed in on my face, as if I reminded him of something he couldn't quite place – "Hello there miss, how can I help you today?"

I smiled, in a rather melancholy way, and simply stated what I wanted. "Can I have the strings changed please?"

I quickly opened the case and he gasped quietly at the instrument inside, gently lifting the violin in his calloused hands as if at any wrong touch it would fall apart. He looked at me again, that lost look in his eyes. I raised an eyebrow, confused about why he was so incredibly fixated with my face.

"I'm sorry if I'm scaring you miss, you just look like a man I served with, is all," he said voice raspy and fragile.

I was taken aback, not sure how to proceed with the conversation as he turned into the back room, to do what I had asked. Anxiously I rolled up my sleeves. It wasn't possible. He couldn't have. What were the chances? Mindlessly, I watched him wander back to the front desk, violin in hand, his foggy blue eyes returning to rest on me again.

"Wilson, you look like Wilson."

I jumped out of my trance as he set the violin neatly back into its case before he continued to talk.

"He had a daughter, she'd be around your age now. He talked about her all the time. You look so much like him the resemblance is uncanny." There were tears forming at the corners of his eyes. "Or maybe I'm just thinking about him too much. It's kinda the day for that, don't you think?"

I looked at the calendar he was gesturing to, I knew exactly what today was – it was the reason I had come here in the first place, a tradition of mine. I reached out to grab the case and he stared at my wrist now exposed as it hovered in place. He zeroed in on the swallow I had had tattooed there recently. I smiled sheepishly, we both knew something that the other didn't want to say. Swallows were his favourite – they were Wilson's favourite.

"No charge miss, have a nice day," he said, smiling to himself. I collected my things, mumbled a quiet thank you and shuffled out the door. I stopped to check the time, reading the watch on my other wrist – eleven. It was at that moment that the rain spontaneously stopped and the sky cleared while a solitary bird flew.

It was a swallow.

Forté

Logan Aldred

In the 14 years I've been alive, I've learned the sound people make when they walk. Sometimes it's a thud thud, or a clack clack; but there's always two beats, one after the other. Step, step, step, step, left, right, left, right.

Also, in the 14 years I've been alive, I know that the sound I make when I walk is vastly different than the basic one-two. It's more, clack, step, swish, clack. No, I don't have two extra legs that make weird noises. My right leg doesn't quite work as it should, so I have two metal poles that help me walk. I suppose you could call them canes, but I don't like that because it makes me sound old.

Of course not all kids have "canes", but I was born with a special symptom called multiple sclerosis that affects the way I do things. At first I couldn't bend my toes the right way. Now it's somewhat evolved; I can't use my legs at all. Don't worry. It's not all bad, I can still use my upper body. Although my fingers are starting to get difficult, and my doctor thinks my eyesight may go soon.

I think the worst part is that my fingers are giving up on me. Besides using them for everything else in life, I use them to play the piano. That's more important than anything. My dream is to get into Juilliard and travel the world playing in a grand orchestra. Yeah, MS is an obstacle, but I'm on my way. My first step is to be accepted into Abstract School of Arts, and in five minutes my audition will be held.

Suddenly, a loud voice rang out over the intercom, "Sylvia Stone, please report backstage, you're up next."

I grabbed the two metal poles from beside me and struggled out of my seat. Slowly, I trudged out of the waiting room and found myself behind the curtains. There was a tall, thin young man sitting on a stool, centre of the stage, and playing the cello to five people sitting in the front row of the auditorium. The audience must be the school directors. The young man finished off his song with a loud screech, and all five of the directors clasped their hands on their ears. The director in the middle cleared his throat, "Thank you Hans. That was... certainly something," he said as he rubbed his ear. "In two weeks you will get a letter informing you of our decision." With a nod Hans was off the stage and it was my turn.

All five directors looked at clipboards on their desk to see who was next. The lady farthest to the right shot her head up and whispered to the others, "But Marcus, she has MS."

There was a pin drop silence. All five adults looked as if someone had just screamed the worst possible curse word. After about a minute, the man in the middle pursed his lips and sighed, "I know, but she paid the entry fee and filled out the forms like everyone else. We have to give her a chance." He cleared his throat once more and called for me to take the stage.

Having two extra metal "legs" basically guarantees that everyone knows when I walk into the room. They also guarantee awkward situations when I meet new people, just like right now. With a final wobbly step I made it to the piano bench and sat down. I swung my legs across the bench and turned to the staring crowd. "Hi.. um... my name is Sylvia. I'm a pianist, and today I'll be performing "Hallelujah" by The Pentatonix, which... uh... they adapted from Leonard Cohen."

The man in the middle wrote something on his clipboard and nodded for me to continue.

I spun back towards the piano, my limp leg hit the bench and caused a loud bang to echo throughout the auditorium. What a great start. I set my poles against the bench and hovered my clammy hands over the keys, they trembled in sync with my pounding heart beat.

"Deep breathing," I told myself. The first key I played shot warmth throughout my arm. The second brought the tingling sensation to my torso, as I slipped my foot on the pedal the feeling shot up my legs. My whole body was soon overcome and I lost myself in the song. My fingers danced along the keys as I told them to, no wavering, no stuttering, just as if anyone else were playing. When I was playing the piano I didn't have multiple sclerosis, my foot steps sounded like everyone else's, and I certainly wasn't losing control in my hands. I was just me, putting my heart into the song.

As the last note echoed in the auditorium the sensational warmth slowly left my body through my fingertips. After playing, reality came back faster than a jet and harder than a truck. No matter how hard I try, the song always ends and I always have useless legs, wobbly fingers, and a progressing disease.

There was a scattered applause from the directors. The woman to the right took a deep breath. "I see you chose to play some parts of the song in forté▢Why did you decide to change the score in that way?"

"Well," I hesitated. "I think it adds emotion, and creates a stronger impact for the audience and myself." That must have been a good answer because she smiled and jotted something down on her clipboard.

The man in the middle cleared his throat again and shot his head upwards. "Why did you chose this song?" he asked intently.

"Um…" This audition was starting to be more like an interrogation. "It's my mom's favourite song, because she says it describes a warrior pleading mercy to a god, and that god granting mercy on the damaged warrior. Apparently, it reminds her of me and my battle with multiple sclerosis. Uh... yeah."

Nobody wrote anything on their clipboards. They all just looked at me like I was about to turn into a unicorn. Finally, the directors thanked me and my audition was over. As my mom and I were walking out of the school, the secretary reminded us that acceptance letters would be delivered in two weeks. That was that. It seemed like the rest of the day went by faster than my audition.

Two weeks seemed to stretch for as long as they possibly could. In the time it took the school administration to decide a yes or no for me, I had five visits to the doctor, three tests at school, learned eleven songs on the piano and had a trip to the hospital. Finally on a grey afternoon, I stumbled out to the mailbox on our front porch. The lid creaked open and revealed three plain white envelopes. The first two were bills, as I flipped to the last one I had to blink a few times to make sure my eyes weren't playing tricks on me. The words, "Miss Sylvia Stone", were stamped along the middle front, and in small font in the top corner was, "Abstract School of Arts".

I ripped open the envelope and unfolded it so the first third of the letter was legible. The plain note read:

"Dear Miss Stone,

We regret to inform you that we cannot accept you into Abstract School of the Arts at this time. We are flattered you chose our school as your secondary education option."

It felt as if someone knocked the air right out of me. I wavered against my poles and leaned on the door to keep from falling to the ground. Out of panic, I ripped the letter open and nervously read the rest of my rejection letter. They had much more to say about why I wasn't allowed into the school.

My eyes darted from line to line, taking in all they let on. Gradually, the corners of my lips curved into a smile, I pushed off the door and hobbled into my living room. Mom was sitting on the couch watching television. I slammed the letter down beside her so she could read what the school had to say. Just as mine did, her mouth rounded into a smile as she grasped the paper which stated:

> *We ask that you join our summer development program at the school to further your musical ability. The program is completely provided by the school and no cost is needed for you to attend. We wish for you participate to gain knowledge in the field you'd like to study. We also ask that with your new skills from the program, you audition for Abstract School of Arts two weeks before the semester begins, on August 28th.*
>
> *It would be an honor if you could join us.*
>
> *Sincerely,*
>
> *Marcus Mason, School Principal."*

Bake Me a Pie

Julia Llewllyn

"Good morning Luciel," my father says, as I groggily enter the kitchen.

"Morning Dad." I run my fingers through my hair as I approach the island in the middle of our kitchen. I pull a plate and cutting board out from one of the drawers. My dad rustles his paper at the kitchen table.

I turn to the fridge and open it, grabbing eggs, cheese and tomatoes.

"Omelette?" I call.

"That sounds great, thanks," my dad answers. I run the tomato under the tap and grab a knife from the drawer on the left side of it. As I head back to the island, my older brother walks in through the doorway. He nods at my father and holds out his hand to me.

"Good morning sunshine," I tease, giving him a sickeningly sweet smile.

"Plate me."

I sigh, grabbing a plate and handing it to him. I chop my tomato and cheese into small chunks, sliding them to the side of my cutting board.

"Abriel, can you grab me a bowl?" I ask. My brother grunts and pulls a large metal bowl from the cabinet above the sink. He passes it to me, ruffling my hair. I swat his fingers away and snatch the bowl. I crack five eggs into the bowl and beat them with a fork.

"Grab a frying pan and pour the eggs onto it," I instruct. "Oh, and don't spill."

"Geez, you're bossy in the morning," he comments.

"Abe," my father warns. I carry the cutting board to the stove where my brother is cautiously pouring eggs into a deep pan. I sprinkle my cheese over the pool of eggs and tomatoes and turn the burner down, knowing my brother would put it on high so he can eat earlier.

I make my way over to the sink and rinse my hands, wiping them on my pyjama pants.

"Set out some glasses and the orange juice. I think there's some left," I tell Abriel. He obliges.

I check on the omelettes, flipping them with a spatula.

"When does mom get back?" I call in my father's direction.

"Next Thursday," he answers, his gaze staying focused on his paper.

After the omelettes are done, I plate and serve them. Both men grunt their appreciation, before devouring them. I almost roll my eyes. We eat, my father reading us snippets of the paper. My head snaps up when he briefly outlines a baking contest.

"What did you just say?" I ask, feeling suddenly excited. He gives me a look.

"Three kittens are for sale at – "

"No, no, before that."

I watch as his eyes scan the paper, retracing his steps. He ruffles it and opens his mouth.

"Frederick's 'Pie Baking' competition. Are you interested in baking for money? Do you want to wow our judges with your creative and delicious ideas? We've got just the place for you! Come on down to Frederick's Farm on June twenty-second and show us what you've got! Prizes include…" I ignore the rest of what my father says as I grin widely. A pie baking contest?

"Luciel?"

I snap out of it, seeing both men eyeing me expectantly.

"O – oh – okay," is all I say. They exchange glances with one another before they both shrug and my father continues reading. June twenty-second.

I excuse myself from the table to go upstairs and call my best friend, Fae. She squeals once she hears the news.

"Oh my god, Luce! That's great!" she exclaims. "You have to let me help you. Besides, you only have a few days before the competition."

Fae's father owns a bakery, and whenever I'm hanging out with her during the summer, we always get to help out there. It was at that bakery where I first learned how much I love to bake.

"Oh would you? That would be great," I praise her, feeling slightly-less burdened.

We make plans for me to come over to her house.

"My dad will totally love this!," she says, more to herself than to me. Soon afterwards, I'm on my way out the door to the bus stop, bag of clothing in hand as I say a quick goodbye to my dad and brother.

For the next three days, I help Fae's dad in his bakery. He shows me how to make a pie crust with the right consistency so it will hold the filling without looking sloppy. We make crumbles and cream pies and even a few meat pies, each one making it out to his display shelves where he tells me, "This one will sell fast."

The night before the competition, Fae's father gathers everyone into the dining room and announces that I'm ready.

"You will do well, girl. I can feel it." he tells me, thumping his fist on his chest twice. Fae rolls her eyes, and I chuckle.

"Alright dad, I think we should get to bed early. Luciel needs her sleep to do well in the competition tomorrow." Fae steps in, grabbing my hand and dragging me up to her room. I smile gratefully at Fae's father before following her.

I toss and turn through the night, my stomach unable to calm down. In the morning, I know I look like I haven't slept in ages. No one comments, thankfully.

After eating almost nothing for breakfast, Fae and I make our way to the bus stop at the end of her driveway. My stomach grumbles and groans and my hands shake as we board the bus.

"Hey, Luce, everything is going to be fine. You'll do great," Fae tells me. I nod and swallow, not trusting her words as much as I know I should. I keep my eyes peeled for the sign that reads, "Welcome to Frederick's Farm".

I've been to Frederick's farm before. We go every year for Halloween to get pumpkins and go through the corn maze. When the farm started selling Christmas trees, we made it a tradition to get our tree from them every year.

"Support the locals!" my mother always tells us. Never, in my whole experience of Frederick's, have I seen so many people here. I have to pry my eyes away from the window so we don't miss our stop.

We thank the bus driver as we get off, and Fae grabs my arm.

"I can't believe I'm really doing this," I mutter to myself, eyeing the number of people who have come here to watch us bake. I turn to look at my best friend. She shrugs.

"I can," she tells me simply and pulls me towards the gates, making me gasp and chuckle.

The people are loud, buying drinks and pastries. I grin so much that after a few minutes, my cheeks begin to ache. I turn to watch Fae, noticing she seems to be feeling the same way.

"We have to find registration!" I shout over the crowd. She nods her head and we speed up, keeping an eye out for any kind of directions to the event. Suddenly, Fae squeezes my arm and points. I follow her finger to a large sign that reads, "SIGN IN FOR BAKERS". My stomach twists and turns faster and I stop in my tracks. Do I really want to do this?

As I stand there, Fae decides for me, signing me in. She drags me towards a large stage, littered with tables and ovens. The world whooshes around me and I faintly feel the pat of re-assurance she gives me as a tall man with a microphone gives us instructions. My throat pulses.

And it begins.

A Little Bit Different

Morgaine McEvoy

One day, in a far away land… just kidding! Hey, my name is Stephanie, and I recently moved to a town called Guelph in Ontario, Canada. It's a nice town and all, but I guess I'm more noticeable in school than ever, which makes me miserable. I have a skin disease called eczema. It's not a crazy, deadly, rare disease or anything. It's actually pretty common, but for me, it's my whole life.

See, I have eczema all over my body, and it's bad. Like really bad. My skin is always red and flaky, and I have to keep my frizzy light blond hair in a bob otherwise it would irritate my neck. My mom had it when she was younger, but now she's really pretty and can have any length of hair she wants. Even though I know it's something I can't control, I still sometimes hate myself because of it. Everyone thinks I have cancer or something like that. And the worst part is, they think if they touch me, they'll get it too. That's not how eczema works!

My dad, mom, and I moved here because my dad got a job at the Canadian Blood Services in Brampton and it was too expensive to move to Toronto. My dad has the night shift; he sleeps all day then is gone all night, so I never really see him. My mom is sort of controlling, but I don't mind too much. She's also kinda my only friend.

I go to Golden Sierra Elementary and I'm in Grade Seven. I get good grades, although I try to never speak out in class. I'm pretty shy and I love musicals. *Newsies* is probably my favourite. I've memorised almost all of the songs and I'd love to play Katherine. She's one of the main characters by the way. She's pretty and gets to be the love interest, and man, would it be great to play her! I'm not a superb singer, but I'm okay. I take piano lessons, so I'm not bad at reading notes and all that.

I only have one friend besides my mom, I guess. I share my locker with her; her name is Ashlyn. She's nice, but sometimes she's a little weird. She'll lash out at me or call me names, but most times it's because I deserve it.

"Hey there, Scaly Steph, how's it hangin'?"

That's her coming now to grab her books. She calls me Scaly Steph a lot, but I don't mind too much. I mean, I am pretty scaly.

"Not much," I reply. Surprisingly, the day goes normally until the announcements.

"There will be a drama club starting! If you're interested, meet in the music room after school." A spark ignites in my brain. This is the chance I need. I can finally meet my people!

At lunch, I meet up with Ashlyn. "Hey, did you hear that announcement? The one about the drama club. Well, I was thi –"

"Oh, don't tell me you were thinking of going to that nerd convention? No wayyyyy. Come on, after school, we can go to my house!" She giggles. I'm trying so hard to say no, I really am.

"I uh, sure but –"

"Cool, see you then!" She walks off. Gosh, why do I do this to myself? Sometimes I feel like my life is a draining bathtub. You know, like at the end of a bath when all the water runs down? Sometimes I wish I could find that plug and stop the water.

* * * * *

On Monday I walk into school, and when I don't catch sight of the usual backpack that Ashlyn owns, I know she isn't here. Yes, I have the whole day to myself! While the thought of Ashlyn not being here makes me happy, I kinda feel guilty too. The day goes normally, although I don't get anywhere near the amount of backhanded comments that I usually get, probably because Ashlyn isn't around. In class, I'm barely listening to the announcements when I hear something that makes me sit bolt right up in my chair like someone taped a ruler to my back.

"The Second meeting of our drama club is after school today! Meeting in the music room." I don't know if anyone is looking, but I'm sure my face is lit up. The rest of the day goes painfully slow, and when my last class is dismissed I run like someone lit me on fire.

When I'm ready, I run into the music room and sit at the back. No one is there yet, not even Ms. Clark. A few people trickle in and they sit in the front. They're chatting and only a few glance back at me and whisper. Finally, the teacher comes in and everything goes silent.

"Hello, everyone. Since we only have a few months 'till our Christmas performance, I would like to do a few more read-throughs today. And – oh!" She looks over at me and I start to panic; man do I hate getting called on.

"Everyone, we have a new member! This is Stephanie." All the kids look at me. They don't have disapproving looks, but they aren't welcoming either. More like, 'you need to prove yourself' looks.

"Stephanie why don't you come to the front seats. There's one for you next to Piper." I look around and get up.

The time flies by and I enjoy myself. We're assigned characters and we do read-throughs. I've never heard these plays before, but they're funny and it's great to play the characters,

When it's over, we start packing up and I feel like I don't look any different than everyone else there. Then it changes.

"Hey, so what do you have?" asks one of the girls, Paige. I look at her and raise an eyebrow. I don't know what the heck she's talking about. "Like your skin." The whole room goes silent. I feel my heart drop.

"Oh, um eczema," I say, turning away from them and slinging my bag onto my back.

"Is it contagious?" She asks from behind me. I feel like a dam; the years of people ignoring me because I was 'contagious' was the water waiting to overflow, and now here it goes.

"Excuse me?! You know what?! It's not! But why would that matter? Apparently, if I touch anyone, they'll suddenly get what I have. Well, you know what? I was born with this and I doubt it will go away soon! So if any of you care to comment on my 'contagious disease' again, I swear I will make your life hell!" I take a breath and stalk out of the classroom.

I regret it as soon as I get out of the school. I know I've spoken irrationally. But I'm just tired of the ignorance. Tired of the uninformed comments. I'm just done. That comment pushed me over the edge.

I have time to think while walking home. What has listening to Ashlyn made me? A boiling pot of rage waiting to spill over? All those insults that I thought I had deserved? Maybe my friendship with Ashlyn isn't as much of a friendship as I thought.

* * * * *

The next day when I get to school, I go straight to our guidance counsellor and ask what to do. She recommends switching locker buddies. So I go to my teacher, Mr. Kester, and ask to switch locker buddies. He asks why, and I explain to him. He simply nods and gives me my own locker.

When I grab my stuff from my new locker Ashlyn comes up to me. "Why did you switch lockers? I thought we were friends!" She says with an almost purple face. I have to keep calm.

"Because we were never friends. You never treated me like a friend or even someone you liked. So, I don't get why you even care," I say as calmly as I can. All she does is look stunned then stomp away. Then another girl comes up to me. It's Paige.

"Hey, so I'd like to apologise for what I said last night, it was so stupid. And I looked up eczema and I know what it must be like –"

"No, you don't," I cut her off. "But," I continue, "I know that you are sorry, so it's okay. I shouldn't have freaked out like that."

"So does that mean you'll still be coming to drama club?" she asks.

"Yeah, I will," I reply, and smile to myself as she walks away.

Defined, Destroyed

Aluki Chupik-Hall

The city streets were bloated with activity deep into the night, but if you knew the right path, you would find yourself in a forgotten area of the town. Cal was somebody who knew the right path.

Cal, more often than not, had returned to this place, and stayed for disconcerting amounts of time, hidden among the rubble and dust. In these moments Cal felt closer than ever to nonexistence.

Cal's first memory was of her perched on a theatre chair, her neck craned so that she could see the stage before her. The arms of the chair were fake wood, coated in a peeling lacquer. With her short legs she kicked at the chair in front of her, anticipation brewing in the very bottom of her stomach. From there, the memory cut off in strange places. All she could recall in between the static and ink patches was a magician disappearing. He fell in a cascade of sparks and smoke from the mortal world into a realm that was not yet glimpsed by people like Cal – or so she liked to think. It was that one moment that made Cal's entire world implode.

Moulding her entire life's course after those few seconds was a hastily made decision, but one she did not regret. Ever since then she had invested every second of her spare time into learning how to dissolve into thin air. And when Cal was ten, she had perfected the art of not existing. She rarely got called on in class when she didn't want to, and she went un-touched when walking through the halls. It was that skill, so deeply embedded in her, that caused Cal to cease to exist one day, with her body pressed against the tile floors, and her head touching the underside of her desk, Apus' hand slipping away from hers. That moment, as her attacker paraded through the array of desks, she was the only one in the classroom who once existed, but didn't anymore.

At least, for a moment.

As Cal began to delve into this knotted sort of witchcraft (if that was an appropriate word for what she had lost herself to) she noticed a previously unexplored alley, identical to the one she found herself in daily. It was in that very spot that she met a girl with misty eyes and a peculiar way of dressing. The girl did not acknowledge Cal for a long while, but simply let her gaze wander into an unknown place in the distance. Although it wasn't very cold, the girl's breath formed in light clouds, which seeped from her lips. Cal did not allow herself to move until a shiver unravelled from the very end of her spine, and travelled through every bone. This was what made the girl finally glimpse Cal.

She uttered only one word: "Cold?" Her voice was mono-tone, yet it seemed to twist and break off in strange places. It cut through the air and rang out for too long, so that even when the girl's lips were once again closed, Cal could hear the word echoing through the alley. Even the one syllable was enough for Cal to conclude that something was very different about this girl.

Cal didn't talk. She hadn't talked for what seemed like an eternity. Yet this girl seemed like the exact person she had been reserving her voice for. Something urged her. Some-thing tugged the words forward and into the frigid air.

"A tad." Cal raked her top teeth over her bottom lip, now al-lowing herself a little more movement. Her throat curled into a tight ball. It was wrong to speak, almost. It was impossible. Yet she had. She just had. She spoke again. "You?"

"I am not familiar with such feelings anymore," said the girl, taking a lock of dull, straight hair in her finger and twisting it absentmindedly. It looked like she was trying to restore life to it. She was failing. The rest of the girl was as flat as her short hair. Her ancient-looking clothes hung limply. Her mouth was a straight, unflinching line. Even when the girl spoke or breathed, her lips showed no sign of emotion. It was an eerie sort of thing. It was an abhorrent hollowness that showed in every gesture. Maybe she was right: she was not manifested by such feelings anymore.

After Cal's life had found a direction, she began to learn through trial and error. One of the less successful methods of drawing attention to herself was a white sheet, which she would drape over her body and then hunch in a corner. From her point of view, the disguise was flawless. Everybody else just thought that she looked like a ghost.

"That's what you are, isn't it?" Cal asked the strange girl the next day with a voice that felt different. Full of gravel and softened by tears. It was a timid thing, the fear of speaking only outweighed by curiosity, which was strange. Cal had forbidden herself from that a long time ago. In this place, though, she couldn't help herself.

Was that good?

"See, that's the problem." The girl said. "I'm not much. People seem to think that ghosts are made of things. Usually, it's just one memory, something that defined us. Something that made us or destroyed us." Cal didn't know what had destroyed the girl, but she knew what had destroyed her. She remembered the scrapes on her elbows and knees, her clothes making chequered imprints on her skin after crouching under her desk for so long. She recalled her voice seizing, like a dog yanking against a chain. She remembered an injured yowl which begun in the back of her throat, and threatened to come up. She didn't know how, but she held it back, just long enough.

"How does it feel to die? Like, what do you see after?" Cal knew it was rude, to ask such questions of somebody she had just met, but it didn't really count, she thought, if that person wasn't really a person at all. Besides, she was beginning to get used to her new found curiosity.

"I don't remember, if that provides any consolation. Just like blowing out a candle, sort of," the girl said in her droning voice. Cal thought that it was a nice metaphor. Not all lives were like candles, though. Some were like forest fires.

Cal knew a forest fire. Apus.

"Were you happy?" Cal leaned forwards.

"I guess I was, when I was living. I had a path, I had dreams that were further away. But, if somebody were to tell me that I was going to die that day, that young, then happy wouldn't be the first word to come out of my mouth." Cal knew that she would say the same. If somebody had warned her, if the boy had ever noticed her eating lunch or sitting behind him in math, if he had told her...

"As would I." Cal felt something strange bubble inside her. It wasn't irritation, but it was close. "It's not something I can change, though. It's too permanent." Like a tattoo, right on her forehead. Trauma girl. Invisible. Hiding under the desk until the math-class boy swinging the rifle passed. Even then, quiet. She had shackled her voice and padlocked her mind. Sitting next to her, Apus.

"Say hello to Apus for me, will you?" Cal knew that something this casual wasn't appropriate for greeting her friend, but she didn't know what else to say. Her words had been spent of ultimately useless questions.

"I will, don't worry." The ghost breathed.

Everything about Apus Phillips was sharp and noticeable, right down to her name. She never stood in the background. Everything else but her always seemed to fall out of focus. Once somebody met Apus, they were completely fixated on her. She finished all her assignments on time, signed up for every after-school club. When her ambition was tugging at its chains, she let it break free. She wore it on every piece of clothing she owned. And, by the time she met the girl who was fixed on disappearing, she was visible to everyone.

It was on the day that Cal picked the best time to disappear, that Apus picked the worst time to stand out. That was her downfall. She was an easy target for the boy, who had quickly found her, even though she was up curled into a ball, even though she was holding her breath. That was what defined her. That was what destroyed her.

The Black Massage Chair

Callista Pitman

Tip sipped her tea, waving to Ali as she walked out of the tea shop.

Mia skipped along next to her. They headed over to the massage chairs to wait for Ali to finish ordering her tea. Tip plopped down in one, watching the mall shoppers go by. Mia crouched down and peered into the change slot.

"Have you ever actually used one of these?" she asked Tip curiously.

"Well, I've never turned one on, if that's what you mean, but I've sat in them plenty of times," Tip answered.

Mia opened her purse and got a toonie. "Well, there's always a first time! Want to try?" she asked.

"Sure!" Tip sat back.

Mia pushed the coin into the slot and the chair whirred. Arm and leg clamps appeared out of nowhere, fastening Tip in.

"What the? I didn't know it did that!" Tip exclaimed uneasily.

"Me either!" Mia rose to her feet.

Suddenly Tip's chair began to lower down into the mall floor.

"No!" Tip screamed, terrified.

Mia scrambled to the edge of the dark hole that Tip was slowly disappearing into, desperately trying to yank her free.

Ali emerged from the tea shop, holding her tea. "Tip! Mia!"

Her tea dropped from her hands, splattering the white tile. She raced across the strangely empty mall, busy just seconds ago. Tip's whole chair was in the darkness when the clamps suddenly sprung open, freeing her. She stood on the chair, reaching up, her fingers stretching. Ali knelt at the edge of the hole, reaching down to her, leaning as far as she dared. Their fingers met for a split second before Tip was pulled away by her descending chair.

"No!" Ali screamed. "No! No!"

"Ali!" Mia grabbed her, pulling her away from the hole.

Ali twisted away, to find that the hole was closing, and Mia had just saved her from Tip's fate. Ali collapsed, sobbing. Mia put her arm around her shoulder.

A policeman tapped Mia on the shoulder, awakening her from her reverie. "Young lady, a store employee just called me, saying he heard screaming out here."

Mia told her story, and the policeman listened silently.

"Girls. There's no need to make up wild tales. Just tell us what happened to the massage chair and it'll be fine," he told them.

"We're telling the truth!" Mia pleaded. "Please, you've to believe us!"

"I think you need to come with me," the policeman said, frowning.

"No!" Ali cried. "We can't leave her!"

"Come with me." The policeman forcefully laid his hands on their shoulders, leading them away.

* * * * *

Tip collapsed on the chair as the floor closed above her. The depressing darkness made her shiver in fear. Her chair finally bumped to a stop.

A fluorescent light flicked on and Tip froze. A man in a white coat with goggles and a surgical mask stood in front of her. Before she could move, arms grabbed her from behind and forced her arms back onto the armrests. The clamps sprung over her wrists again.

"Must've malfunctioned," a gruff voice said. The scientist, as she decided he must be, stood in front of her and produced a huge syringe. Tip's mouth went dry. She felt a stab of pain and then all went black.

When she woke, she was in what looked like a jail cell. She was alone, but in the cell next to her was another girl who was alarmingly pale. And in yet another cell nearby paced something that looked like a wolf, but was somehow not a wolf.

She curled up in the corner and began to cry.

"Who are you?" The voice was ghostly, coming from the cell next to her, the one with the pale girl.

"T – Tip." Tip stuttered nervously. "Who are you? Where is this? What – what will happen to me?"

"Calm down. My name is Maria. I have been held captive here for three weeks now. Nothing much happens except we occasionally get taken out of these cells and they take some of our blood." The girl held up a hand. "That's why I'm so pale. We get food once a day. Usually porridge or something like that."

Tip groaned. "My head hurts." She cradled her head in her hands.

Maria nodded sympathetically. "Happened to me too the first day. Probably fear and loss of blood. Try to get some sleep."

Tip obediently curled up in a corner of her cell. Tears ran down her face as she tried to sleep.

A man opened the cell door cell, waking Tip. He wore the same coat, goggles, and mask as the man who had stabbed her with a needle. Tip shrank into the back corner of her cell, heart hammering, but the man walked in, picked her up, and slung her over his shoulder. Tip didn't struggle, knowing it would be of no use, and fearing the consequences if she did.

The man deposited her in the same chair as she had arrived in, and the clamps sprung over her again. Tip gritted her teeth, trying to think of anything to help her get out of this torture chamber. Suddenly she recalled how the clamps had come loose as she descended in the chair, and desperately tried to remember what she had been doing when that happened. It came to her: she had been trying to unscrew the screw that attached the chair to the clamps. The man began to push the chair (Tip had not realised it had wheels) down a long hallway.

They came to a stop in a room where another scientist was positioning Maria in her chair. Maria's eyes were squeezed shut. The man pushing Tip's chair went over to that scientist and they had a quiet conversation, not noticing Tip's arm clamps spring open.

Tip rose from her chair, and walked silently over to stand behind the men. Maria's eyes blinked open, and widened in surprise to see Tip standing there. Tip held her finger in front of her lips. Maria closed her eyes once more. Tip wound up, her heart pounding, and punched the man in front of her with all her might. He toppled to the floor like a toy solider. The other man's eyes barely had time to widen before he too was knocked out by a strong punch to the jaw.

Tip raced over to Maria, and showed her how to open the clamps. They started to run back down the hall. Suddenly, another massage chair began to lower from the ceiling. Inside, clutching each other, were Ali and Mia! They explained how the policeman hadn't believed them, and how they'd escaped and run back over to the massage chairs.

"Help me find the keys," Tip pleaded, searching around.

"I know where they are!" Maria cried. "This way!"

She led them around the corner, and grabbed them off a hook on the wall. "I saw them once when they were moving me."

The four girls raced back towards the cells, unlocking all the ones with people inside. They left the strangely swollen creatures in their cells.

The people swarmed toward the area where the massage chair that Mia and Ali had arrived in was. Maria arranged a line to get in it, hoping they could get it to rise again. The first two people climbed in, and as soon as their weight was on it, it began to go up. They climbed out as it reached the mall, and the chair sank back down.

Two more climbed on, and then two more. Tip could only imagine the chaos in the mall as the people arrived.

On a table she saw some papers and began to flip through them. Shocked by what she found, she called the others. "It looks like they were injecting human blood, combined with all of these ingredients, into animals to make them stronger and more human-like."

"That must be what those animals back there were," Maria said, shaking her head sadly. "How cruel."

Finally the four girls were the only ones left. They climbed into the chair together, and it rose to the mall. A scene of wonderful chaos met them. The police had found another entrance once the first escapees arrived and had placed the scientists in handcuffs. Mia and Ali just barely resisted smugly saying, "We told you," when they saw the policeman who had doubted them.

The news had gotten out, and people were calling names and crying as they found their missing loved ones. As the friends headed for the door, Tip looked at the massage chairs sitting so innocently in the centre of the mall, and shuddered.

As they pushed through the crowd, Tip glanced back at the massage chairs, and vowed to never sit in one again.

Cursive

Teviah Abman-Dowdell

It was a rainy fall morning. I looked out the window to see my parents packing up our rusty station-wagon. We were on the way to the airport where I was to board the plane. In the four months that preceded, our house was filled with nothing but silence and solitude. My parents were both busy at something; as for me, I was starting to cause trouble. My grades slowly started to drop as I lost any hint of motivation. It was as if my old cheerful self had been stolen from me and shredded into a million pieces. Although I barely spoke a word to my parents anymore, they still knew something was up. Instead of trying to talk to me about it, they booked me a plane ticket. I was to spend six long and dreary months with my aunt and uncle in Ohio.

"Eloise, come downstairs. It's time to go, "my mother said.

I brushed back my long, brown wavy hair and secured it with a bobby pin. This was it. The last I would see of my room for six months. I took one last look at my computer, the thing I was forbidden to bring because apparently I always had my "head in the clouds" and spent all my time writing. But they didn't understand. Writing was for me an escape. I could picture myself in a completely different world with brand new surroundings. Before I left my room, I took one last look at my window seat where I had spent countless hours, engrossed in novel after novel. I packed a few of my favourite books but nothing compared to the library in my room.

"Coming," I replied coldly.

As soon as I got into the car, I immediately plugged my earbuds into my phone and turned up the music full blast. I hoped my parents would get the message that I wanted to be left alone.

"Eloise, take those things out of your ears right now, "my father barked. I sighed as I paused my music.

"We wanted to talk to you, sweetie," my mother said softly. Her voice always sounded lost, somewhere else. It was if she was a ghost, not even there.

"What about?" I responded.

"Your mother and I feel like we need to set some ground rules for when you're in Ohio," my father said. Oh no, not the dreaded lectures. I was used to this. I took a deep breath, in an attempt to prepare myself for the long talk ahead.

"We don't want you treating your aunt and uncle like how you treat us. I—we, expect you to treat them with respect and try to always be positive," my father said.

"Also, we expect you to get your grades up and drop your attitude," my mother added.

"We're not kidding here, young lady. Do you understand?" my father asked.

"Yes, I do," I said.

After my lecture was finished, the car ride was silent and ghostly, like most days at home. I looked out the window, as the rain poured down, wishing I could get my parents to understand exactly how I felt. I imagined myself standing up to them and telling them how sending me away wasn't going to do any good. I wished I could tell them what was going on at school, how I lost my best friend, and how much I deeply needed them. They had never understood me, treated me as if I was an inconvenience. I was aching to talk to them, but for some reason I couldn't bring myself to speak of such topics.

The rain outside the car window continued to fall. Silence continued to fill the interior. The road was slippery, as winter was just beginning to approach.

My father then broke the silence and said, "We just wanted to tell you, Eloise, that your mother and I wrote you a –"

Before he could continue, the wheels of our car started to skid.

"Hold on, Eloise!" my mother said.

We were spinning round and round. At this point I was unaware of my surroundings, and all I could think about was getting out of this car. Then suddenly, I heard a crash and everything went black.

When I woke, there were at least ten people peering down at me, holding some peculiar looking tools.

"Where am I?" I hollered, as I sat up quickly.

"You're at the hospital, you've been in a car accident but you are going to be okay. Please rest your head back down," said a woman in a white surgeon's coat.

My mind suddenly went to my parents. Were they okay? This whole accident had been my fault! By now, I was hyperventilating. The doctors had to help me back down, and eventually I found myself in a deep sleep once more...

The piercing, bright light of the hospital room wasn't the most comforting thing to wake up to. I sat up only to find myself in a tiny bed on wheels. Where was I again? Before I could do anything else, a doctor began to approach me.

"Hello, Eloise. I'm Doctor Hastings. I understand you've been through a very traumatic accident, but I assure you that you'll be perfectly fine."

"Where are my parents? Are they okay?" I replied.

As a nervous look spread across her face, I could tell that something was terribly wrong. I felt as though my whole body went numb and I couldn't breathe.

"Eloise, I'm afraid your parents did not prove as lucky as you," Doctor Hastings replied.

I had a terrible feeling in the pit of my stomach. Tears began to pour out of my eyes like an overflowing bathtub. Doctor Hastings put her arms around me and pulled me close. I then realised how much I needed that hug.

Later that day, my grandma came to pick me up. She and my aunt and uncle had decided between themselves that it would be best for me to stay with her. As I returned to my grandma's condo with her, I couldn't help but feel guilty. I felt as though I had wished this upon my parents and somehow made it happen. I had no more tears left to cry.

Back at school, I gained some strange sort of popularity. I was soon known as the kid who lost both her parents. People would pass by in the halls, staring at me with looks of sorrow. Eventually, I decided I would try my best to block the incident out of my mind. And that worked, at least for a little while.

* * * * *

It's been three months since the dreadful accident. The ground is beginning to thaw as winter is nearly over. Today is the last day of school before March Break. I take the elevator up to my grandma's condo only to find a mysterious package waiting outside of the door. I pick it up and discover that it is addressed to me. I unlock the door and sit down to open the package. Inside is a letter with a red crest stamped on the outside. A sticky note is attached to the front of the envelope.

The sticky note reads "Dear Eloise, this is a letter from your parents that they intended for us to give you at the end of your visit with us. We thought you should have it. Best wishes, love Auntie Mel and Uncle Scott." I'm intrigued yet nervous at the same time. I trace my finger along the red crest of the letter, admiring its beauty. Then, I finally open it.

Dear Eloise,

We know our family hasn't been on the best terms recently, but we're really hoping that will change. We truly believe that having some time apart will help us all heal. Although it might not seem like it right now, we want you to know that we love you so much and have always wanted the best for you. You're our special girl, and we know that we will push through as a family. We hope that you'll go on to great things with that amazing mind of yours. Never shoot any lower than your biggest dreams. We are and will always be so proud of you.

Lots of love,

Mom and Dad.

My hands tremble as goosebumps begin to creep up my back. Tears stream down my face. I hold the letter close to me, and take a deep breath. At that moment, my grandma walks in and puts her keys down.

"Is everything okay, sweetie?" she asks.

"Yes, I'm alright, thanks."

She pulls me in close, as tears pour down my face.

"I love you so much, grandma. I want you to know that," I tell her.

"Oh, Eloise, I love you too," she says.

Lights Out

Liam Engel

Do you ever find yourself invisible, ignored, or of little importance? That's where this story begins, an outsider coming into new land, suspicious land. Though suspicious, it is most definitely the most gorgeous land in the world, or is that just a cover up for something else entirely?

"Wow," whispered Keith as he and his mother drove into the new city, Élando. He didn't know where the name came from, but he didn't give much thought to it either way.

They were crossing a large grey stone bridge into the new city. From where they sat in their heated car seats, they could already see their apartment building. It was a beautiful glass building with twelve floors, and they were on the tenth floor. Keith didn't really feel like moving, but he liked the idea of living in an apartment building.

"You ready?" Keith's mother asked, an uplifting smile on her face as she turned her head to look at his smile in the front seat beside her. His tanned face contained a small pattern of freckles on each cheek. Past his freckles, his curly hair fell down to his shoulders. His mother's face was an average tan with no freckles, and her hair a dark brown just past her shoulders with the same slight curl as Keith's.

"Yeah, yeah, I'm ready." Little did Keith know that this was the most important day of his life. He would some day soon bring justice to the mystery of the great big city.

Here it is, thought Keith, as he walked with his mother through the apartment's front doors. They approached the front desk and his mother received the key to their room as he looked around the lobby. He saw furniture everywhere. The colours made it look like a showroom, the chairs and sofas being grey, brown, and orange. He then found something that caught his attention. A painting hung at the far left of the room. It was of a man sitting on a chair pointing with his right hand at something, but the painting didn't show what. "Odd," Keith murmured to himself.

"Alright," spoke Keith's mother with the same smile as before.

She walked towards the elevator doors. The doors opened almost the moment they reached it, and they hopped in it almost the moment it opened. Keith's mother pressed the number 10 button.

"Mom, I thought that this was a twelve floored apartment," said Keith, as he eyed a button that had the letter z on it.

His mother looked at the button he was staring at and answered, "Hm, I don't know."

The elevator doors slid open and they hopped out. Keith looked to his right and saw the shiny glass. He was glad to see that it wasn't transparent because that would only add to his doubts about their new place.

The carpet that they walked on was fuzzy black with a few dirt stains.

"Here we are!" exclaimed Keith's mother as she slid their room key in the rusted bronze lock. Pushing the door open, Keith's mother flipped the switch to her right and the yellow light came shining down on them. Keith dropped his bag that he was carrying in the front hall and jumped on his bed. He felt as if he could fall asleep in his jeans and red t-shirt.

That night Keith and his mother slept without trouble, until some strange and far away noise disrupted Keith's sleep.

"Destrooy!" Keith rolled in his sleep. "Destrooy!" The voice grew louder, but he still ignored it. "DESTROY!" Keith jumped in his bed on account of the voice rising to a scream.

Keith jumped up from his bed and slipped on his shoes in the front hallway. He opened the door and shut it behind him, slow and careful, not to wake his mother or anyone else in the hallway.

He heard a scraping noise like nails on a chalkboard, except harder. He followed the noise down another hallway, identical to the one he lived in. It had the same black carpet, but there were no stains, almost as if it had been purposefully avoided by the people living there. It had the same perfectly carved wooden table in the centre of it with the yellow table cloth across the middle. On the table stood a single candle in the centre. The flame was as wild as the building was tall.

Keith turned to his left and hopped in the elevator. After it opened he ran as fast as possible, noticing that the noise was getting quieter. Once nearly at the source of the sound he was stopped. There was a door in front of him that had the letter z on it. Keith tried opening it but it was locked.

"Beep! Beep! Beep!"

It was the alarm awaking Keith and his mother at seven o'clock. Not knowing that this was the day everything would go right in the city, Keith lazily turned the alarm clock off. He had quickly gone up to his room once discovering that the door was locked.

Keith thought that maybe it was all just a dream, a fake reality, but it was as real as anything could get within the city of Élando.

"Mom, mom," whispered Keith as he shook his mother attempting to wake her up. He finally succeeded and got ready to head out for their walk around the city.

They hopped in the elevator closest to them, which was the one that Keith had been in not too long ago. Keith reached out to press the lobby button, but stopped. Z, what floor is z? Keith asked himself, now pressing the lobby button.

"You okay, darling?" his mother asked, placing her hand on his shoulder.

"Fine," Keith answered, just as the elevator doors slid open.

They began their walk by heading north, right from their apartment building.

"We'll head downtown to grab breakfast," stated Keith's mother, taking his mind off of things. Following his mother, Keith passed by more buildings. The one to his right now was a short glass apartment lined with a streaky black border. They crossed the cleanest intersection Keith had ever seen. It didn't have any scrap or paper on the smooth gravel. I guess that's just one of the many reasons Élando is the finest city, Keith thought to himself.

Keith followed his mother into a small brown cafe. As they opened the door the bell above it gave a scratchy ring. Keith grabbed a seat while his mother bought breakfast. When his mother returned she sat opposite to him in a nice brown chair.

Keith began eating his food in silence. "What's wrong?" asked Keith's mother, digging into her breakfast as well. He was just about to answer when something caught his eye. It was a painting, in fact, it was the same painting as in the lobby of his apartment. Keith pulled away from the table and walked over to it. It was the exact same, even the frame was. Keith put his arm in front, slowly walking closer and closer to the painting until he was millimetres apart.

"Keith?" Keith turned around to see his mother behind him. "What are you doing?" she asked, her once continuous smile faded.

"I was just looking at the painting, I –"

"Painting? Keith, that's a wall."

"I –" Keith began but stopped. What did she mean it was a wall?

"Keith, honey, are you okay?"

Keith slowly nodded his head and headed back to their table. I'll wait until she's asleep. I have to find out more about that painting, planned Keith.

So the day went on, and so did Keith's curiosity.

It was a little past ten when Keith was sure his mother had fallen asleep. He quietly got up from his bed and slipped on his shoes, same as before, and headed down to the lobby. He carefully crept past the person at the front desk reading a book and found the painting. Just as before, he put his arm out and slowly walked closer. His cold fingers touched the painting.

A flash, Keith arose from a cold cement floor and looked around. Behind him was the same door with the letter z on it as the night before, and there, the same screeching as the night before. He followed it down the empty corridor and found a door that made it look… not so empty.

The noise was definitely coming from within that room. Keith pushed open the door and found the source: a black coat hung over someone.

Gathering all of his strength, Keith spoke in a voice almost as shaky as a whisper. "H – Hello?" As soon as his words fell out of his dry lips the figure turned around making Keith jump.

This couldn't be right…

Another flash, and the lights… burned out.

www.ingramcontent.com/pod-product-compliance
Lightning Source LLC
Chambersburg PA
CBHW052206170626
46812CB00004B/1667